Thunder Rolling
in the Mountains

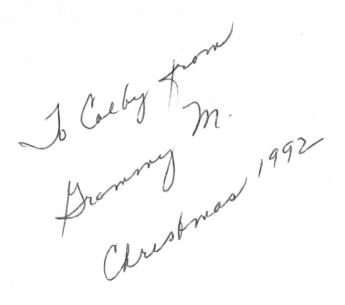

To Colby from
Grammy M.
Christmas 1992

Thunder Rolling in the Mountains

SCOTT O'DELL AND
ELIZABETH HALL

HOUGHTON MIFFLIN COMPANY
BOSTON 1992

Library of Congress Cataloging-in-Publication Data

O'Dell, Scott, 1898–1989.
  Thunder rolling in the mountains / by Scott O'Dell and Elizabeth
Hall.
    p. cm.
  Summary: In the late nineteenth century, a young Nez Perce girl
relates how her people were driven off their land by the U.S. Army
and forced to retreat north until their eventual surrender.
  ISBN 0-395-59966-0
    1. Nez Perce Indians—Juvenile fiction. [1. Nez Perce Indians—
Fiction.   2. Indians of North America—Fiction.]   I. Hall,
Elizabeth, 1929–   . II. Title.
PZ7.0236Th   1992   91-15961
[Fic]—dc20   CIP
                        AC

Printed in the United States of America

BP   10   9   8   7   6   5   4   3   2   1

To Susan

Also by Scott O'Dell

Foreword

At the time of his death, Scott O'Dell was immersed in the story of Chief Joseph and his people. Their courage and determination in the face of cruelty, betrayal, and bureaucratic ignorance moved him deeply. So deeply that he continued to work on the manuscript in the hospital until two days before he died.

A few years earlier we had followed the trail taken in 1877 by Chief Joseph and his valiant band, from the beautiful Wallowa Valley in Oregon to the bleak battlefield at Bear Paws in Montana. From that trip, from the recollections of Nez Perce and U.S. Army personnel, from the writings of historians, and from Scott's instructions and musings about the story, I have completed the manuscript, as Scott had asked me to do.

Most of the characters are based on actual Nez Perce, and most of their words and deeds are drawn from recollections of survivors. Swan Necklace is based on three warriors: Strong Eagle, Yellow Wolf, and the historical Swan Necklace. Essential to the book's existence are the two eyewitness accounts compiled by Lucullus V. McWhorter: *Yellow Wolf: His Own Story* (the recollections of Chief Joseph's nephew) and *Hear Me, My Chiefs!* (based on eyewitness accounts of both sides), as well as *Chief Joseph's Own Story,* which he told on his trip to Washington, D.C., in 1897. Other helpful books are Merrill Beal's *"I Will Fight No More Forever": Chief Joseph and the Nez Perce War,* Helen Addison Howard's *Saga of Chief Joseph,* and Arthur Josephy Jr.'s *The Nez Perce Indians and the Opening of the Northwest.*

Elizabeth Hall

Thunder Rolling in the Mountains

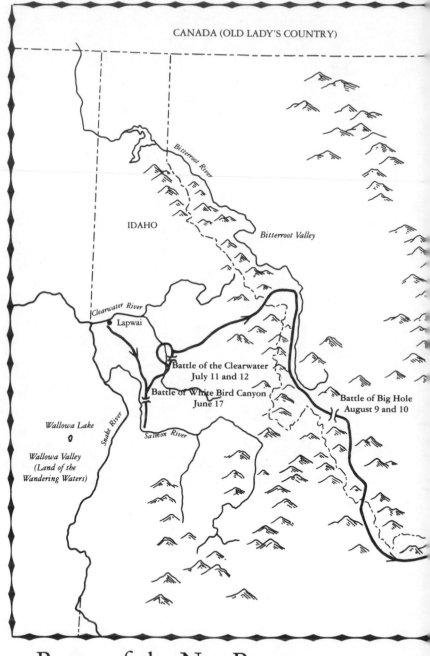

CANADA (OLD LADY'S COUNTRY)

IDAHO

Bitterroot River

Bitterroot Valley

Clearwater River

Lapwai

Battle of the Clearwater
July 11 and 12

Battle of White Bird Canyon
June 17

Battle of Big Hole
August 9 and 10

Wallowa Lake

Snake River

Salmon River

*Wallowa Valley
(Land of the
Wandering Waters)*

Route of the Nez Perce

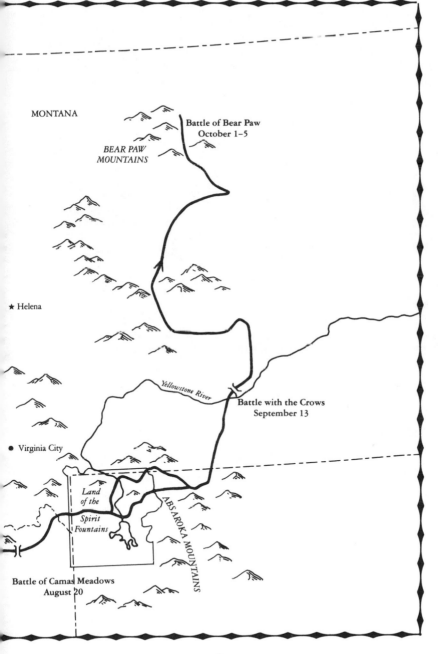

MONTANA

Battle of Bear Paw
October 1–5

BEAR PAW
MOUNTAINS

★ Helena

Yellowstone River

Battle with the Crows
September 13

● Virginia City

Land
of the

Spirit
Fountains

ABSAROKA MOUNTAINS

Battle of Camas Meadows
August 20

June - October, 1877

One

THAT DAY we dug roots in Deer Meadow. Now we were riding fast for home.

There were seven of us on good horses. I rode in the lead, pulling a travois filled with cous roots. We were on a trail of fallen trees and rock slides, but a storm was coming and it was the shorter way to our village.

I had not ridden the trail for many moons. It had changed a lot in that time. We came upon row after row of fallen trees, trees too jumbled for the travois, and I was forced to go around them.

We came to a treeless spur on the mountain. A north wind blew down from Hawk's Peak. It was spring but the peak was covered with snow and the wind whipped the snow down upon us in wet clouds. It was hard to see the trail.

"I am freezing," Little Lark, one of my cousins, said. "I think we should go back and take the long trail."

The other five riders, two of my cousins among them, agreed with her, but the girls sat on their horses and said nothing.

"There's no hurry I know about," Little Lark said. "We told our mothers before we left to dig roots that we would be gone three suns. The third sun is somewhere in the mist. It will be above us when we reach home."

I gave her my blanket and we rode on and left the mountain spur. The trail dipped down out of the wind into a place of tall grass and a winding stream. It was a beautiful meadow. I remembered riding through it at the beginning of winter when the aspen trees had turned to gold.

The aspen trees were gone. Their branches were lying around, but the trees were gone. They had been sawed off close to the ground.

I saw smoke rising at the far end of the meadow. It came from a cabin made from the aspen trees.

We pulled up our horses and sat staring. The horses were nervous. They raised their heads and sniffed the air. We were more nervous than the horses.

"What is it, Sound of Running Feet?" asked my friend White Feather.

"White people," I said. "Indians do not build cabins."

Many times when our chieftains talked I heard them speak of the white people. They had not set foot upon our land, only on the land that belonged to a part of our tribe, those who called themselves Christians, those who had sold their land to the Big Father, who lived in a faraway place called Washington. The white people were called settlers and they came to plant seeds, but mostly to dig gold out of the streams and the rocks.

I cautioned my cousins and the other girls to ride at a trot and to keep their eyes to themselves. None of them had a weapon, but I carried a rifle. My grandfather Old Joseph had given it to me more than six snows ago, as he lay dying. Until my fourteenth birthday, three moons ago, it had hung in the lodge. Then I took it from its place, for I, Sound of Running Feet, was then a woman.

In this short time I had learned to use it. At first it was too heavy to lift and I had to prop it up on a branch or on my horse's back before I could shoot. Now I could handle it and shoot straight. My father did not like the rifle. But Old Joseph had given it to me. It would be bad to speak against the gift now that Old Joseph was dead. He could come back and make trouble.

Three children sat in the cabin doorway. When we rode by, they were as quiet as mice when an owl is around.

Our trail crossed the stream a short way beyond the cabin. A man and a woman with her hair piled on top of her head stood in the stream up to their knees. The woman was shaking a copper pan, letting the stream wash over it. The man kept filling the pan with dirt that a boy of our people brought him in a shovel.

The woman kept working when she caught sight of us, but the man stopped. He was tall and thin and had a scraggly beard and a small bald head. He said something I did not understand, which the boy changed into our words.

"He wants to know how you are," the boy said.

I paused with the others silent behind me and did not answer his question. I said, "Ask the white man why he has built a cabin on land that he does not own."

The boy I knew about. He showed Ne-mee-poo tattoos on the back of his hands. He had gone to the mission school near the Snake River, at Lapwai, the Place of the Butterflies. His name was Storm Cloud and he had been mixed up in a murder.

I asked him again. He looked at me with anger in his gaze before he spoke to the white man.

The white man said, and Storm Cloud changed his words, "You Nez Perce own too much land. You can't use all the land, not half of it, not even a tenth of the land. You are a greedy bunch."

The whites called us Nez Perce, although that was not our name. They said it meant "Hole through the Nose." None of our people ever put ornaments in their noses, but when the whites decided something was so, nothing could change their minds.

All of us were angry. We glared at each other. Then the man warned us not to send our warriors to talk to him.

"If you do there'll be trouble," he said. "My name is Jason Upright and I have friends."

I pressed my lips tight to hold back the words. Then I dug my heels into my pony's sides and we all rode through the stream and across the meadow.

There was a tall hillock at the bottom of the meadow covered with trees. As we came to the top, I jumped off my horse and took careful aim with my rifle at the pan Jason Upright's wife held in her hands. The shot made a big hole in the pan and tossed it high in the air.

Our trail followed the winding stream and crossed it many times, so we had trouble with the travois piled high with kouse roots. We also came upon a bear, a grizzly bear, standing in the middle of the trail, eating berries from a juniper tree.

He stretched up taller than I did sitting on my horse. We waited at a distance until he had eaten all the berries he wanted. Yet we reached home before the wind storm swept down from the mountains.

Two

AT DAWN the wind no longer blew from Hawk's Peak. It blew from all three of the towering peaks, down upon our village. No fires burned outside that morning because of the wind. I went through the great lodge and divided the kouse roots we had gathered.

I told my father about the white people who were living in a cabin on one of the creeks that fed Wallowa River, how they were digging gold. I said nothing about the hole I had shot in the woman's copper pan.

"They're the first, but more are on the way," he said. He often talked to me, for he had no sons. Unlike other girls in our village, I often talked back.

"We will stop them. Here we stand," I said. I felt angry when I thought of white people cutting the trees and planting wheat where our horses and cattle roamed.

"No, daughter. We're few and they are many. They're locusts and they'll devour us."

"Not if we stand and fight."

"If we fight, they will devour us all the quicker." My father turned his back, which meant that he would not listen to another word. His mind was made up. "I do not like this wind," he said. "It sounds like many horses running."

Joseph, my father, son of Old Joseph, was an honored chieftain of the Ne-mee-poo. He was their chieftain because he could see far away into the land of the suns and moons that had not yet risen. At the snowflakes before they fell. The small green worm deep in the ruddy apple. The thought before it is spoken. He was a kind, gentle man, for me too kind with the whites. He was not a warrior.

"On the backs of the running horses are soldiers," he said. "Their leader is Howard."

"The man who has only one arm?" I asked.

My father nodded.

We were standing among some trees on the shore of Wallowa Lake. Waves piled up on the shore. Stout trees thrashed and bent. The mats around the bottom of the lodge flapped like birds ready to fly away.

My father stood tall and broad-shouldered. He had black hair that he wore in two long braids tied with ribbons. He used to play games with me, but not anymore. Not since the white men had come to root gold from our hills and streams and I had stood with those who would fight.

"Why does the white leader return?" I asked. "You answered him once. You spoke plain words to him."

"He returns because he does not believe what I told him."

"Now you'll tell him again?"

"This time he rides with soldiers."

"But still you will tell him?"

My father did not answer. His silence made me afraid that at last, at last he would weaken and give in to the soldiers.

A single horse ran swiftly toward us. On its back was Too-hul-hul-sote, an honored priest of the Dreamers and leader of the rovers from the Seven Devils country. He was in Wallowa to speak with my father about the soldiers.

"They come," he called. "The one-armed general leads them."

"I know," my father said. "I hear their horses."

The sun was dying as we stood beside the lake. In the last of its light a band of soldiers rode out of the woods. They came fast through our village. Out in front rode General Howard, the man who had one arm and wore silver stars on his jacket. He pulled up in front of us and a soldier came out and stood beside my father to help the two men talk together.

8

"As I rode through your village," the general said, "I looked but saw not one sign that you plan to heed my order and move your people from Wallowa."

My father answered him in a gentle voice. "We have decided not to move to Lapwai, this other place. It is small and far away. It has little grass to feed our many horses."

"You have a thousand horses, Chief Joseph," General Howard said. "You have thousands of horses. You have more horses than you can ever use or sell."

My father said, "I have been to Lapwai to look. There are Indians living in Lapwai already. I saw three lodges and many tipis."

"I will move them," the one-armed general said. "Everyone will be moved and there will be much room in Lapwai."

"That is not good, to drive people from their homes," my father said.

A furious gust of wind bore down upon us. The general's beard blew straight out. The two men stood and stared at each other.

In a tangle of trees behind them, three men, two of them in red jackets, were watching. They had ridden up silently. I knew all of them. The Red Coats were warriors who had sworn to fight General Howard and his soldiers to the death.

Their leader was Wah-lit-its. He hated the whites because his father was murdered by a white man, who had never been punished for the crime. Red Moccasin Tops, his cousin, hated the whites for the same reason. They lived for the day they would take revenge. They wore their red jackets as a warning sign to the whites of the revenge that would come.

To one side among the trees stood a tall young man, his hair piled on top of his head and a leather band painted with flying birds tied tightly around his forehead. Swan Necklace was cousin to both Red Coats but was there, I knew, only to guard their horses.

He didn't hate the soldiers or the white settlers, or anyone else, not even his own father, who called him an idler and sometimes knocked him down with a sharp cuff on the ear. He would get to his feet again, brush the dirt from his jacket, and smile.

The last time his father, old Two Moons, gave him a thrashing I was watching. It was three suns ago, early in the morning. Swan Necklace had been away all night in the mountains. He went to the mountains to gather baskets of earth, all colors of earth, yellows and reds and blues.

He mixed the colors with something that looked like water but was really a secret of his own, and painted pictures of the sun and moon, of birds and deer and buffalo. He painted the pictures on dresses and jackets, on mats and skins if the owners wanted them. The paint never rubbed off or faded.

As soon as Swan Necklace slid off his horse the morning he came back from the mountains, his father grabbed the baskets of earth and scattered them on the ground.

"Listen, idler of all the hills and valleys and meadows in this realm of the living," he said. "Listen to me."

His son listened and smiled a little, but more to himself than to Two Moons.

"Death stalks the Land of the Wandering Waters," his father said. "We are surrounded by soldiers who are here to drive us from our homes or to kill us. Our young warriors—you know them all, many are your relatives—have armed themselves and stand ready to face the soldiers, to die! And here you come riding in from the mountains with dirt to paint pictures."

He gave Swan Necklace a shove that sent him sprawling. He stood over him and said, "I gave Red Moccasin Tops and Wah-lit-its the blankets from which they made their red jackets. Now I give them my son to take care of the horses. I have spoken to them. They will accept you as a horse holder. Go now to talk about horses."

Swan Necklace got to his feet, but he hung back and did not leave us.

His father said, "You have no choice. Go or I'll banish you from the clan. You will be a wanderer for the rest of your life, no longer a Ne-mee-poo."

Swan Necklace glanced at me. We had grown up together. I had loved him for a long time, for as many moons as there are stars. I put a hand over my heart and gave him the secret sign of love.

Without a word, he went off to talk to the Red Coats.

Three

THE WIND swirled high in the treetops. The one-armed general let go of his beard. My father unwrapped the light folds of his blanket.

The general said, "Tell me, chief of the Wallowa Nez Perce, one whose intelligence is praised by friends and enemies alike, tell me, do you believe that I have spoken to you before and speak to you now with two tongues?"

"With one tongue only," my father said. "And I too speak with one tongue. Believe me when I say that we do not wish to move to Lapwai."

"I believe you, Chief Joseph. So you must believe me. I say again to you and to your clan that you must leave Wallowa."

My father thought hard. His mouth was closed tight and his hands were pressed across his chest. He glanced at the snowy peaks, at the blue lake, and at the green meadows fading with the sun.

"You do not understand that Wallowa is my home. And you do not understand why."

The general was not listening. He said something to one of his soldiers, who smiled, but my father did not notice. I noticed and held my breath in fear.

"When I had lived on this earth for ten snows," my father said, "in this beautiful place that surrounds us, I climbed that mountain." He paused and pointed to the mountain with both hands open. "High up, where I could look beyond in all directions, I made a bed on a stone. I had no water and no food. I closed my eyes. I put a pebble in my nose and a pebble in each ear to keep me awake. I floated far beyond the sky, far beyond this world.

"Five suns I lay there, my stomach on the cold stone, my mouth burning with thirst. I began to wonder how many suns would rise before my guardian spirit came and spoke to me."

The general still was not listening. My father went on. He was talking more to himself than to the general.

"I wondered if my guardian spirit would come. If he would leave me nameless and alone because I was unworthy of being a man.

"Then without a sound, out of a quiet night, he came. I could not see him. Whether he was young or old I cannot say, but clearly I heard him speak a name.

"I climbed down happy from the snow mountain. Other young men, my friends, had also gone to the sacred place and were given names. We chanted our names until the moon went down and the sun came up.

"I have many names, but Thunder Rolling in the Mountains is the name that binds me forever to this Land of the Wandering Waters."

"I am tired of talk," the general said. "I have heard enough talk. You and your people will leave Wallowa before thirty suns come and go."

Too-hul-hul-sote was walking up and down, staring out from the folds of his blanket. He was a huge man with a fierce eye and a rumbling voice.

"Who are you to tell us what we must do?" he said to the general. "You did not make these mountains. The Spirit Chief made the mountains. He made the streams and meadows, the trees, the grass, the beasts that eat the grass and the birds that weave it into nests. The Spirit Chief made everything. Who is this man that will tell us to leave our home, our mother, and go to a place that does not belong to us?"

"I am that man," the general said.

My father moved between them. I am sure he feared that the hot words would end in a bad fight. Once, when the general first came to Lapwai, he fought with Too-hul-hul-sote, put chains on him, and locked him up in the soldier's jail.

"I can't move my people to Lapwai now," my father said. "The Snake River is flooding. We would need to cross from one shore to the other through torrents of water. Many of my people are women, children, and the old. I have thousands of cattle. Half of them would be swept away."

The general pointed a glittering sword at my father. "Listen," he shouted. "I have heard enough excuses. Now I speak my last words. If you have not moved your tribe from this place before thirty suns have risen and set, then I shall send soldiers with guns to drive you out."

My father drew his blanket close about him. "I hear your words," he said. "I carry them to our people. In thirty suns we will be gone. There must be no blood."

General Howard nodded his head. He did not smile, but there was a glint of pleasure in his eye. He motioned to a soldier. The soldier blew a trumpet and the band galloped off. My father watched them cross the meadow, splash through the stream, and swiftly disappear.

While he watched them and said nothing, I saw the Red Coats scramble out of the bushes. Swan Necklace was waiting with their horses. He got on his own horse and the three of them rode off. I knew where the Red Coats were going. Swift as arrows, they would ride to the village and tell all they had heard. They would say that Chief Joseph had given in to the one-armed general. They would say that Too-hul-hul-sote had stood up to the general. Every word he had said would be said again.

The young warriors would listen to my father, for they loved him, but they would not obey him. They would never leave Wallowa. They would follow Too-hul-hul-sote to death if that is where he led them.

This was good. The idea of being driven away by soldiers to a strange place far from the home I loved made wild thoughts flash through my mind. I saw myself riding into the soldiers' camp with a torch, setting fire to their tents. I saw myself take aim with my rifle and shoot a soldier from his horse. I saw another soldier running across the meadow, and I shot him too.

Four

FIRE BURNED in front of the council lodge. Our people were gathered around it, talking together. As we rode up, a deep silence fell upon the clan. Most of them would obey Joseph, their chieftain. All but the young warriors would follow him faithfully no matter where he led thm.

He stayed on his horse. "Listen to me with your hearts," he said to them, raising his voice against the wind. "You have heard the sad news. You know we must leave our home. Some among us, the young warriors, will say to you, 'Do not leave. Do not flee like old women. Fight. We shall live here in peace.' "

Everyone moved closer to him. "Now," he said, "many soldiers camp on our lake. As many as we have warriors, and they all carry guns. At Fort Lapwai hundreds of them wait. To the east and to the west more soldiers are waiting, many more. To escape them would be dodging hail in a hailstorm."

The people pressed closer to my father. They were terribly quiet. They felt the truth of his words, like heavy stones falling upon them.

From somewhere in the trees, Wah-lit-its called out, "Sitting Bull, the great Sioux chieftain, did not run. He fought Custer. He killed all of his soldiers."

"But where is Sitting Bull now?" Chief Joseph asked.

There was no answer from Wah-lit-its.

"He's far away," said my father, "hiding in Canada, the Old Lady's country."

"It would have been best had he stood and fought," said Two Moons. He stumped up and down, swinging his cudgel. "There would not be so many white soldiers."

"But there *are* too many white soldiers. So many, we must go," my father said.

Ollokot, my uncle and the best of the warriors, nodded. "You speak the truth," he said. He picked up a cherrywood bow. "This bow looks strong," he said, "but it cannot stand against someone stronger." With a quick movement of his massive hands, he snapped the bow in two.

My father held up his hand. "In ten suns we leave Wallowa. Make bundles of all you value. We will not return, not for a long time. What you leave behind white scavengers will steal."

My mother looked sad. In a few weeks she would

have a child. She wanted her child to be born in our Land of Wandering Waters. Many times she had said this. At my father's words, she sighed once, a deep sigh, but she made no protest.

The people waited for my father to say more. When he was silent they wandered off to the lodge. I heard no cries and no weeping. They had swallowed their tears.

A moon came up and the wind faded away. It was a time for love songs, but there were no sweet songs, only the beat of drums.

Before I went to bed I talked to Swan Necklace. The Red Coats had gone and he was guarding their horses in front of his father's lodge.

"You have heard Chief Joseph speak," I said. "Where do you stand?"

"I go with Red Moccasin Tops and Wah-lit-its," he said bravely.

"You guard their horses, but where are your weapons?"

"It is important to guard their horses. And I have a knife."

"But you do not carry it."

"It is hidden in the lodge."

"Why is it not in your belt?"

"I forgot to put it in my belt."

"It's dangerous to ride around without a weapon.

You're no longer a painter of pictures. You're a fighter against those who want to kill you."

"I don't feel like a fighter."

"You will when someone shoots at you."

"Do you believe that the Great Chieftain high above will protect me when someone shoots?"

"You must think so, then you'll be brave."

He got up and put his paints away. He was painting a blanket for our wedding.

Everything had been done for our wedding, or almost everything. First Two Moons and his wives had come to talk to my mother and father. They brought many presents—horses, blankets, wooden spoons, and an iron kettle.

They asked Chief Joseph and Springtime whether I wished to marry their son. My mother came outside where I was hiding, listening under a bush, and asked me if I wanted to marry Swan Necklace.

"Yes," I said.

"Do you love him?"

"Since longer than I can remember," I said.

There was more to do before the wedding could take place. Chief Joseph and Springtime had to give presents to Two Moons and his wives, and Swan Necklace had to finish my buffalo blanket.

I asked Swan Necklace about the blanket.

"I talked to my father last night. He was angry that

I even thought about a wedding. He said that there was a war to be fought. He said young husbands make poor warriors."

"That means we can't be married until the war is over."

"Not until the one-armed general and his soldiers are driven from Wallowa, my father said."

"Wait," I said.

I went to the lodge and brought back my rifle and a pouch of bullets. Swan Necklace stared at the rifle as if it were a snake.

"I don't know how to shoot," he said.

"Red Moccasin Tops will teach you," I said. "He will show you how to lie flat on the ground behind a rock. How to lie flat and shoot and push the rock ahead of you. How to ride low to one side of your horse so you can't be seen by your enemy and shoot under the horse's neck."

The booming voice of Two Moons called his name. Before he could move, I put the rifle in his hands and slung the pouch of bullets over his shoulder.

Five

WE WERE on the banks of a mountain ravine. Snow water from many streams poured into the Snake at this place. It came roaring down in a yellow flood. Waves reared up and heavy mist filled the air.

Here, Ollokot took command. He was very tall and had his hair cut in a roach that stuck up and made him look like a giant. He put a guard on the herds at night and circled them himself.

Soldiers camped above us on the side of the riverbank and built fires. They watched to see that we crossed the river. They did not offer to help us.

My father said, "If General Howard had let us wait until late summer, when the water is low, then we could cross safely. Now we must struggle."

"Lose cattle and horses and risk our lives," Ollokot said. "They brought us here to drown. They plan to get rid of us forever."

Ferocious Bear, a shaggy warrior from the Seven

Devils country, spoke up. "We should not move from this shore," he said. "The soldiers wait there on the mountain to see us swept away. Let us stay and kill them."

"Kill one and ten will take his place," Chief Joseph said.

Too-hul-hul-sote sat on his spotted pony gazing at the river while the other chiefs talked. His restless pony pawed the ground.

When they fell silent, Too-hul-hul-sote gathered air in his huge chest and shouted. He spoke to the one-armed general, wherever he was.

"Our Great Spirit Chief made the world," he said. "He put me here on this piece of the earth. This earth is my mother. You tell me to live like the white man and plow the land. Shall I take a knife and tear my mother's bosom? You tell me to cut the grass and make hay. But dare I cut off my mother's hair? The Spirit Chief gave no man the right to tell another man where he must live and where he must die."

His voice trailed off. The leader of the white soldiers did not hear him. My father and Chief Ollokot, his brother, did not hear him. They did not listen to him, nor did Tall Elk and Ferocious Bear. The decision had been made to cross the river.

"Now we build rafts for the crossing," my father said. "And boats."

"Gather our herds," Ollokot said. "More than two

hundred cows have been driven off by the whites since we came to the river and half that many horses. We'll lose many more before the sun rises again."

"We go at dawn," Chief Joseph said.

Too-hul-hul-sote's eyes flashed but he said nothing more.

That night we built fires and by their light made rafts and boats for the crossing of the Snake. Men cut alder trees and bound them together with leather thongs. The rafts were strong but hard to handle. The women made bullboats from willow frames and buffalo hides stretched tight. Bullboats look like melons cut in half. They swirl round and round and bob like corks, yet they are safe in the rushing water.

As the sun came up, our five bands gathered at the riverbank. In my father's band from Wallowa, the Land of the Wandering Waters, there were sixty-two warriors and three hundred women, children, and old people. The warriors were naked except for breechcloths. Their bodies were covered with thick bear grease to keep out the cold and they wore red feathers in their braided hair.

Chief White Bird, who was very old, brought a band that was next in size to my father's band. It had fifty-one warriors and two hundred and fifty-five women, children, and old people. They came from White Bird Canyon, beyond the river.

Chief Looking Glass was there. He was a great

warrior, not as tall as my father. His black braids were streaked with white and their tips wrapped with brass wire. He wore brass rings in his ears. A round-looking glass always hung from a rawhide around his neck. Looking Glass brought forty warriors and two hundred women, children, and the old. They had lived peacefully in a small hidden village on the Clearwater River, yet white miners had found them and treated them badly. They had killed their cattle and stolen their horses.

The smallest of our bands belonged to quarrelsome Too-hul-hul-sote. There were fewer than fifty of these Palouses, but their warriors carried good rifles and were the best buffalo hunters among all the Ne-mee-poo.

The night was long. Gathered on the bank, we waited for the sun. It came up bright and lit the hills where the soldiers were camped.

It took a long time, half the morning, for the sun to find its way down the dark canyon walls. It lay on the river in shimmering sheets that blinded us. We couldn't see the river because of the fierce light, so the chiefs decided to make the crossing late in the day.

When the light changed, Ollokot sent out riders to herd the horses close to the river. Chief Joseph stood at one end of the herd, Ferocious Bear stood in the middle, and Ollokot on his big stallion stood at the other end.

Ollokot fired his pistol. The riders shouted. The frightened horses stampeded into the river and swam for their lives. All of them got to the far shore. The cattle were next. Warily, they walked into the shallows, but the riders forced them into the river. Half of the cows and all of the spring calves were lost.

Ollokot sent out rafts loaded with the things we had saved clothes, ornaments, buffalo robes, lodge skins, packets of gold dust, bags of kouse mush, dried berry cakes, camas roots, and smoked meat and salmon wrapped in deerskin.

We lost only two rafts. The soldiers watched from the hill but did not offer to help.

The sun moved down in the sky. In its rays the rushing water sparkled like a river of jewels where Ollokot gathered our people. The old women, the old men, and the children were placed on rafts and lashed down. Babies in cradleboards were strapped to their mothers' backs.

One end of a stout rope was tied around the waist of a horseman, the other end to a corner of a raft. In this way, with a horseman at each corner, and the horses plunging against the swift water while their riders clung desperately to their backs, our people crossed the river.

Three of us were left to go, Chief Joseph, my mother, and myself. One star shone above us. The dark river turned to silver. I had made a bed of buffalo skin for my mother. It was warm but she complained of the cold. She got up and wrapped a robe around herself and went down to the river.

Fires were burning on the far shore.

"It is time to go," my father said.

Springtime did not answer. She lay down again and pulled the robe over her head.

My father got out the last of the bullboats and I made a bed for my mother in its bottom. He picked her up to put her in the boat, but she slipped from his grasp and went along the bank to a big rock that jutted over the river.

"This is no time for play," Chief Joseph said.

"I am not playing," Springtime said. "I will have my child here before we cross the river. This is my home. This is Wallowa. Over there where the soldiers watch and fires burn is not our country."

"It will be our country soon," my father said. "It is better that our child be born where his home will be."

He edged toward her and talked softly.

Her back was against a rocky ledge that hung over the river. He moved closer talking softly, ready to take her in his arms. The ledge was slippery with spray and she was heavy, but before he could grasp her she clawed onto the ledge, out of his reach.

She sat above the torrent, looking down at him. Her hair was wild with spray. I think that if he had tried to follow my mother she would have thrown herself into the river. If she had, I would have followed her.

"How long do you sit?" Chief Joseph said. He was not pleased. He was not used to being defied, not by his wife. "Already you shiver with cold. You will be sick. The child will be sick. How long does this madness last?"

"Until the child is born," my mother said.

"After we cross the river," Chief Joseph said, "it is yet a march before we come to Lapwai, our new home."

"In my heart," she said, "this is my home. Not over there on the far side of the river."

"And in my heart, also," I said to her.

I said this under my breath, but Chief Joseph heard it. He walked away, gazed for a while at the raging river, then came back. He asked me to build up the fire. In a gentle voice he spoke to Springtime and she came down from the ledge.

As the sky grew light in the east, her child was born. At dawn we got into the bullboat and horsemen guided us to the far side.

Six

NOW WE WERE on the far side of the Snake, and Chief Joseph took command of our people. We climbed out of the dark canyon to an aspen grove, where the herds were allowed to graze. Then we set off toward Lapwai, our new home.

We went to the Salmon River and crossed it safely because we had crossed the mighty Snake already. At Rocky Canyon we camped beside a pond surrounded by aspen trees. Twenty suns had risen and set since we crossed the big river.

"Lapwai is near," Chief Joseph said. "We can reach it with a short march and obey General Howard. But before we go there'll be songs and dances, horse races and games to mark our last days of freedom."

Everyone agreed with him, especially the young warriors. The feast days were loud with the hoofs of racing horses, the nights with the throb of drums and the soft cries of flageolets. On the last day before we left there was a parade of all our clans. The horses wore beaded harnesses and their finest saddles. Colored streamers fluttered from their manes and tails.

I didn't go to the parade. Bending Willow, my new baby sister, was sick and I stayed to help Springtime take care of her. I had built a fire to make a kettle of kouse mush. Night shadows lay on the meadow where we were camped, when Swan Necklace rode up to the fire. Braids of his long hair hung wild around his face. He opened his mouth but couldn't speak.

"What has happened to make your tongue go to sleep in your mouth?" I asked him.

"War," he stammered. "War!"

He wanted a drink of water and I brought it. "War? What war?"

"With the white soldiers. Wah-lit-its started a war."

"What do you mean? How can one boy start a war?"

"Wah-lit-its was riding fast through the camp, having fun with Red Moccasin Tops," Swan Necklace said. "By accident his horse stepped on some kouse roots that belonged to Sour Tongue, who never has a good word for anybody. The old man shouted at him, 'See what you do. Playing like a brave, you ride over my woman's hard-worked food. If you are so brave, why do you not kill the white man who killed your father? Or are you happy just riding your dead father's horse like a child?' "

"The old man spoke the truth," I said. "That's what Wah-lit-its has done, riding around like a child."

"He rides no more," Swan Necklace said. "Not after the insult. Crazy, he jumped down from his horse and was about to kill the old man. Ferocious Bear took his knife away and threw him to the ground."

"Listen, you saw all this or someone told you? They made up a story and told you."

"I was there. I saw it. I saw Wah-lit-its lying on the ground, crying. Suddenly he jumped up and rode off and came back with his rifle. Then I heard him scream, 'Watch! You'll see I am not a child playing warrior. You will be sorry for your words.' He fired once in the air, then galloped away."

"Wah-lit-its rode off alone?" I said.

"Not alone. Red Moccasin Tops and I rode after him. We caught up with him at the shack where Larry Ott lived. The door was locked. We broke it down but Larry Ott was not inside. Then we went to Richard Devine's place. He's the one who set his wild dogs on any of our people who walked by his house. He once murdered a Ne-mee-poo who was crippled and could not walk. He will kill no more of us. We surprised him. Never had one of the people entered his house. Wah-lit-its shot Devine with his own gun."

"You helped him do the killing?"

"No, not Devine. I was outside, holding the horses. But together we killed another white man who had whipped some of our people with a whip that had an iron tip. And we would have shot the bootlegger Sam Benedict if his bride hadn't begged us to spare him."

Swan Necklace was suddenly calm. "I need more bullets," he said.

I had a pouchful hidden away under the bed in my father's tipi.

"Give me all you have," Swan Necklace said. "There will be much fighting."

"Don't do any more shooting until Chief Joseph comes back," I said. "He's gone off to hunt with his brother. He'll be back today."

"You don't know when he comes back. Things won't wait. Those who need killing will get on their horses and get out of the country, like the white man Ott who killed Eagle Robe."

He drank half of the water I brought him and held out the rest for me. "Drink," he said, "you look pale as a fish belly."

I drank the water. Swan Necklace had changed. He was fierce for war. If I'd had a guardian spirit, I'd have thanked it on my knees.

"Bullets," said Swan Necklace.

Beyond the lake I caught a glimpse of my father

and Ollokot in their black eagle blankets, riding slowly toward our camp. Swan Necklace saw them, too.

"Hurry," he shouted. "My friends are waiting. They're also out of bullets. We have powder but we need bullets."

My father and Ollokot rode at a gallop. They had heard the news of the killing from someone.

"Hurry," Swan Necklace shouted again.

I ran fast to the tipi, took the bullets from their hiding place, and hung them on his shoulder. They weighed him down.

Chief Joseph and Ollokot came out of the trees and up the trail. They galloped to where we stood. They looked grim.

"We have heard that you have killed white men," Ollokot said to Swan Necklace.

"We did," he answered. "We killed two."

"Killing I feared," Chief Joseph said. "It's what I have fought against since the beginning."

"It's war," Ollokot said.

"A war we cannot win," my father said.

He pointed a finger at Swan Necklace. "Remember this, young warrior. None of the soldiers will be scalped. Not one. Remember this yourself and tell what I say to your friends."

Swan Necklace tried not to flinch. He was standing beside the two most powerful men in the tribe. His carbine was stuffed under one shoulder. He looked like a soldier but I think he wanted to run.

Warriors had gathered at the lake and built a fire. Two Moons rode among them, leading the roan horse that had belonged to one of the white men. He called to his son. He held a red jacket above his head.

Swan Necklace rode to his father's side. He took the jacket and put it on. Then he shook his rifle. A cheer went up.

"It is time to fight," said Two Moons. "We will be children no more."

"We will never go to Lapwai," Ferocious Bear said through closed teeth. "Let the soldiers know we will kill them all."

Women began to take down the tipis. Our camp was unprotected, and the soldiers would soon be upon us.

"No!" shouted Joseph. "Let us stay here until the army comes. We will make some kind of peace with them."

But no one listened.

Seven

THAT NIGHT our warriors were called. The old men
and women packed their few things. At midnight we
left our camp and started south for White Bird Canyon, the home of White Bird's band. At dawn on the
fifth day, we came to the crest of a canyon of brush
and rock. This was White Bird Canyon, a place where
we could stay while we decided whether to fight or
flee. We knew the land and our chiefs thought it was
the safest place to camp.

"If the whites follow," said Too-hul-hul-sote, "we
hide and shoot them down as fast as they come."

Streams ran through the big canyon. Water trickled
against stone walls. Beyond us on the cliff we posted a
warrior to watch for the soldiers. All that day and all
that night we waited. My father did not sleep.

At the first gray light a scout rode into our camp.
"Soldiers coming close," he called. "Many soldiers."

My father rose swiftly. He spoke with the other

chiefs. "We must not shoot first," he said. "Maybe they come with good hearts." Ollokot agreed.

The chiefs sent out a truce party. Five warriors rode to meet the soldiers. One of them carried a white flag to say that we did not wish war. The other young men waited on their horses, hidden behind the buttes.

From our camp, we heard a bugle. Then a rifle spoke. The lone shot echoed against the stone walls. There was a long silence, then the sound of guns. A warrior rode into a streak of daylight on the crest of the canyon. He waved his bow above his head.

"War!" he shouted. "The soldiers fired on our white flag."

"Here we stand!" Ollokot shouted. "We go no farther. First we die, then we die again." Ollokot, with his good plans and bravery in battle, was our most cunning chieftain.

Chief Joseph disagreed. "We should hide until night and then slip away. There are too many soldiers. They will kill half our family." My father always thought of his clan first. There were not many of us.

Ollokot divided the warriors and sent them along the hillside. I watched them go, dodging behind the huge stones. I watched Swan Necklace. He rode with the other Red Coats, no longer afraid to fight. My heart beat proudly. I wanted to ride with him.

Instead I took a group of children into a sheltered place beside the creek, where we could play games and forget the bullets flying on the other side of the butte. We held contests to see which ones could hold their breath longest. I smoothed off a flat rock and some of the boys spun tops, making them dance across its surface.

Red Owl, Ollokot's son, started a game of wolf. He pretended to be a wolf and the other children pretended to be calves who had strayed from their mothers. He crept behind the bushes along one side of our sheltered place. The other children pretended to be grazing while they waited for his attack.

But Red Owl did not burst out of the bushes to frighten the others. Time passed. I moved quietly to the bushes and looked over them. There was no one to be seen. Red Owl was gone.

I put one of the older girls in charge of the little ones and began to look for him. I knew he had left to watch the battle. Red Owl had seen only seven snows, but he itched to be with the warriors.

I climbed the butte. Lying on my stomach, I looked across the battlefield. Horses were running in every direction. I saw one horse—its saddle stained with blood—dragging a Blue Coat whose foot was caught in the stirrup. Crossing a low ridge in the distance was Red Owl. Five horse lengths in front of him lay a dead Blue Coat. Beside his outstretched hand was a shining bugle.

I called Red Owl, but he did not stop. He wanted

the bugle for his own. As he reached it, our warriors mounted a charge. They rode past the bugler, and Red Owl was lost from view.

Heedless of gunfire, I flew down the butte. When I reached Red Owl, I dropped to the ground beside him. He had taken cover behind the bugler's body. He was afraid to move. So many bullets struck around us that my eyes smarted from the dust.

As our warriors' bullets and arrows found their mark, the battle moved away. The shouts and gunfire grew faint. Red Owl raised his head and grinned at me. The bugle was clutched tightly in his fist.

I got to my feet and grabbed his arm. My heart still beat fast. "Foolish child!" I said, as my fear turned to anger. "You will be the death of us."

His face grew solemn and he was quiet as we walked back to the camp. He would not be so boastful in front of the others. It was bad enough that the children would admire Red Owl's daring. I did not want them to copy his pranks.

At last the battle ended. We were badly outnumbered, but Ollokot drove our warriors. He made them believe that they were truly fighting for their lands and lives and gods. None of our people was killed, and only two warriors were wounded. By nightfall we had forced every Blue Coat to flee, and thirty-four white soldiers lay dead upon the ground.

There would be more battles with the Blue Coats,

Chief Joseph promised. "They will follow us. We cannot hide. They will find us wherever we go."

Looking Glass said that we must cross the mountains and travel to the land of the Crows. Howard could not bring his big guns over the mountains. We could live in peace with the Crows and hunt buffalo. The other chiefs agreed.

My father was not happy. "This is your fight, not mine," he said. "I will look after the women and children and old men. You must keep the soldiers away."

We left White Bird Canyon and the beaten soldiers. I felt like singing. My pony stepped lively through the grass. Flowers were blooming under the oaks and huckleberries. I rode in the gray dust with the children, behind all the old people.

I made a doll for my baby sister with a piece of a soldier's shirt. The youngest Joseph, nephew of Old Joseph, had found a soldier's knife and was chasing Red Owl. My small cousin had a pair of soldier's heavy boots and asked me to cut off their tops and make a purse out of them.

Beside me rode White Feather, who had watched me shoot the copper pan from the white woman's hands. She was a year older than I. "Are you pleased?" she asked. "The warriors have won and your father has lost."

"I am pleased," I said. "We have beaten the Blue Coats. If they follow us, we will beat them again."

There was a whoop from the children. Young Joseph had caught Red Owl and was sticking him in the chest. I took the knife away from him and when I came back Swan Necklace was riding with White Feather. My pony fell in beside them.

"Were you frightened?" I asked Swan Necklace.

"Just at first," he said. "Then I knew that my guardian spirit would keep me safe. Wah-lit-its and Red Moccasin Tops rode beside me. We charged the soldiers. Two Moons and the other warriors followed. Many of them had only knives or bows." His eyes sparkled as he told of the battle.

"The bullets sang like bees around us, but no one was hit," he said. "We hung to the side of our horses where the Blue Coats could not see us and shot from beneath the neck. Our guns and arrows found their mark. The soldiers stopped shooting. Their horses went wild and tossed them on the ground. They dropped their guns and ran for their lives."

I clapped my hands with joy.

"I have plenty of bullets now," said Swan Necklace. "And all the warriors have rifles. The soldiers won't need them anymore."

Eight

WE FOUGHT the white soldiers again on the banks of the rushing Clearwater. This time many Blue Coats died and we lost four warriors. Six other of our young men were hit, but only one had a bad wound. A soldier's bullet went in the back of his shoulder and came out through his chest. He was shot when he rode his horse close to the Blue Coats to show he was a brave man. But he was strong and continued to fight.

More than a moon had passed since the battle at White Bird Canyon. The soldiers still followed, but we moved fast, so fast we had to leave our cattle behind.

Looking Glass took us out of the valley and high into the mountains. We traveled toward the rising sun and the country of the Crows. The way was hard. Spruce, hemlock, and pine grew close. The trail was narrow and dark. It twisted up the steep mountainside. Boulders choked the path and sharp rocks cut the horses' feet. Trees felled by spring storms blocked the way.

At night we camped. We lived on roots we dug from the ground and bark we peeled from the trees. When cooked in water, the bark made a soft mush that filled the stomach. Some nights we went to bed hungry. The ponies grazed on the bushes and stiff wiregrass.

Five of our warriors stayed behind to scout the back trail for soldiers. The Red Coats scouted the trail ahead. My heart was with them, but I helped dig roots, pound bark, and care for the children. Bending Willow now smiled when lifted from her cradleboard.

It rained every day. As we neared the top of the pass, the path grew steeper. Here it was so narrow that we had to get off our horses and lead them. We pressed against the mountain, moving slowly along the edge of the cliff on a carpet of pine needles. Far below us, a stream wound between rock walls. The trail was slippery, but none of our ponies stumbled.

At last we reached the summit and started down the other side of the pass. The rain stopped and the sun came out. We reached a place beside a creek where hot springs came out of the ground. Steam rose from the rocks. Where the water boiled out it was so hot you could not keep your finger in it. We bathed in shallow pools below the rocks where the water was not so hot. We stayed in the water until we could no longer bear its heat. Then we ran to the creek and plunged into the cold current. The water washed away our weariness.

That day our tipis stood in the high grass. Bushes that grew here made good tea, and we gathered leaves to take with us. There were so many fish in the stream that we called it Salmon Creek. We would have a good meal that night. Water lilies grew in small ponds nearby, and after I washed my hair I twisted a white flower into each braid. I thought the lilies would make a pretty design for moccasins.

As I thought about where I could get some soft deerskin and porcupine quills, the Red Coats rode noisily into camp. Wah-lit-its drew up beside the men who were mending bridles.

"Soldiers in front of us!" he said. He was out of breath and had to rest between words. "Building fort! They will head us off."

Swan Necklace rode to my side and slipped off his horse. "There is danger," he said. He drew me close to him. "The soldiers know our camp. They have drawn logs across the trail so that we cannot pass. They are building a fort. We may have to fight."

"This time I will fight, too," I said. "There are many guns now. I know how to shoot."

Swan Necklace shook his head, "Your father would never permit it," he said. "Fighting is for warriors." He forgot that only two moons ago, he had been a painter and I had possessed the gun. He never spoke of his colored earths now, and he had not painted on our marriage blanket since we left Wallowa.

"Fighting is for those who would stand against the white soldiers," I said.

Before I could say more, the chiefs left the camp to meet the soldiers, taking the Red Coats with them. Looking Glass, White Bird, and Chief Joseph rode in front. My father carried a white flag. Swan Necklace, Red Moccasin Tops, and Wah-lit-its followed behind, in case the Blue Coats opened fire.

It was dark when the peace party returned. The people crowded about them. They heard how our chiefs had stepped off their ponies and walked up to the barricade with empty hands, leaving their guns on their saddles. The soldiers were surprised at their courage, and no one shot at them.

"We told the chief of the Blue Coats that we had only friendship for the people of Montana," said Looking Glass. The firelight flickered on his strong face. "Our quarrel is with the soldiers in Idaho. The white captain shook our hands, but told us we must lay down our guns and give up our horses."

The warriors began to mutter. "I will never give up my gun," shouted Two Moons. He sat on his war horse, looking ready for battle.

"Never," said Too-hul-hul-sote. He struck the earth with his war club. "We did not want this war, but we will not let the Blue Coats take our rifles and horses."

"I agree," said my father. "We cannot do that. But their leader promised no one will attack us if we keep the peace. I advise that we go without talking more."

"There is a way," said Looking Glass. "Once we get past the soldiers, we are free to go into the valley. Before the sun rises, we will be gone."

We ate quickly, then made ready to leave this peaceful spot. We took the buffalo skins from our tipis, but left the poles behind to lighten the load. Cooking fires were smothered, coals raked, and earth heaped over them.

The long line of horses moved away from Salmon Creek. We climbed the steep hill on the northern slope of the canyon, went around the soldiers, and soon were high above the barricade. Trees screened us, but the Blue Coats saw us pass. They did not speak, but they did not shoot, either. The war was over.

Nine

WITHOUT FEAR we followed the creek into Bitterroot Valley. Our march slowed. The scouts no longer
searched the trail for signs of Blue Coats. We moved
through the valley, trading gold dust and horses for
supplies. The settlers seemed friendly. The shop-
keepers opened their stores and sold us flour and coffee, sugar and tobacco. They sold us heavy cloth to
make tipis, for some of our people had left their buffalo robes on the other side of the mountains. We saw
no soldiers. As we rode along, settlers waved at us and
wished us well.

Yet my father's heart seemed to grow heavier with
each step of his horse's hoofs. We were moving farther
and farther from the Land of the Wandering Waters.

Digging my heels into the sides of my spotted
pony, I rode to his side. His eyes looked at the line of
trees where the sky met the earth, but he did not see
them. There was pain in his gaze.

"Are we safe, Father?" I asked.

"Safe for now," he answered without turning his head. "We have left the war behind us in Montana with our enemies. But we will never see our home again. My heart is sick, and I fear to die in a strange land, far from the bones of my father and mother."

"We can still fight," I said. "The blood of our people has been shed, and the young men are ready to die in battle."

My words made him look at me. "Do not talk like that," he said. "The white settlers are like the sands of the river. No matter how many we kill, more come. Our warriors would die and so would many of those who do not fight. And who would care for our women and children when the warriors are dead? They would still be far from home. We must protect our women and children, even if it means we are strangers in the land."

His mouth made a straight line. His words came like a sigh. "We will go on to the land of the Crows," he said. "There we can hunt buffalo and replenish our herds. The Blue Coats do not bother the Crow."

At first I was sad. Then like a ray of sunlight, a thought came into my head. If the war was really over, Two Moons would let the marriage go forward. I began to feel happy. When we reached the Crows, Swan Necklace could find colored earths and paint our marriage blanket. Then we could have our own tipi. When my father felt better, I would speak to him about it.

I dropped back to ride with the children. I showed them the squirrels scampering up the trees and leaping from limb to limb. I pointed out the hawks that hung high in the sky and the woodchucks sitting beside their holes. I called out when we passed patches of ripening blackberries. I told them about the wire strung on poles beside the trail.

"See the silver wire," I said. "It talks all day and night. It sings like a lark, sending the settlers' words from one town to the next."

The children's laughter rang out for the first time since we left Salmon Creek. They did not believe that a wire could send talk across the miles. I found it hard to believe myself, but my father had told me about the click-clack. He said that the clicks ran through the wire like evil spirits, telling the one-armed general which trails we took and where we camped each night.

Swan Necklace joined us. We rode side by side, our legs touching. I looked at Swan Necklace and thought about our marriage and my cheeks turned scarlet.

To hide my embarrassment, I told the children stories about Coyote, the trickster with magic powers. One of their favorite stories was about the time Coyote created the tribes. One summer in the days before there were people, Coyote learned that a fearsome monster was eating all the animals. Coyote went to the river where the monster lived and let the terrible creature eat him, too. Once Coyote was inside the monster's belly, he started a fire. With a stone knife, he cut the monster's heart from its body. As the monster lay dying, Coyote slashed open its belly and freed all the animals.

Coyote cut the monster's body into pieces and flung them across the land. Each piece of bloody flesh became a tribe. One piece became Flathead. Another became Crow. Another, Sioux. Another, Assiniboin. Another, Blackfoot. Another, Kutenai. Another, Bannock. Another, Cayuse. Another, Paiute.

All the pieces were gone when Fox told Coyote that he had forgotten to throw a piece of the monster in the land beside the river where he had killed it. Coyote picked up the monster's heart and sprinkled the land with its rich blood. The drops of blood became Ne-mee-poo, the real people. Coyote never threw away the monster's heart and liver. To this day, you can see them, two huge stone mounds, in the center of our country.

Another time Coyote and Black Bear got into a ferocious argument. Coyote was busy fishing when the argument started. He became so angry that he marched out of the river and threw his fishnet way up the hill. Then he grabbed Black Bear by the scruff of the neck and shook him hard, saying he'd teach the bear not to bother him while he was fishing. He picked up Black Bear and threw him against the hill on the other side of the river, using his magic powers to turn the bear into stone. And there they remain to this day, high above the Clearwater, the net on one bank of the river and the bear on the other.

I told stories until the shadows fell and we came to a halt. We had been in the valley for ten suns.

Ten

WE HAD COME to a second vast valley of brush and willows and tall white trees. A clear stream ran silently from one far shore to another, a day's slow journey on horseback. Blossoms were scattered through the tall grass waving beside the water. We were tired from our long travels and the old people stumbled at every step they took. But the Red Coats strode through the camp with their chests out and their red jackets taunting those who would dare to stop them.

Looking Glass said we would stay at this place for three suns. Here we would cut tipi poles and let them dry. Birch trees with tall, smooth trunks grew everywhere along the shores. They were the best trees for tipi poles. Our women cut down stacks of the saplings, peeled them clean, and set them out to dry in the sun. Without them we would have had to sleep beneath the stars. We would need the poles during the rest of our flight.

We gathered food to eat along the way. The warriors hunted antelope and black-tailed deer, and the old men caught fish. The women dug roots. No one thought of the white soldiers we had left behind in Montana. No one except Lone Bird, one of our brave warriors.

He rode through the camp, telling the chiefs that we must stay on the trail. "I do not trust the Blue Coats," he said. "Maybe they are close behind us. Keep going. Move fast. Death may be following on our trail."

Wah-lit-its agreed. He told of his dream. "Last night I saw myself killed. I do not turn back from death, but first I will kill some soldiers. My brothers, my sisters, I am telling you, we are all going to die."

He offered to take the Red Coats and scout back along the trail.

White Bird said that was good, but Looking Glass told Wah-lit-its to hunt antelope instead. "The Blue Coats are far away across the mountains," he said. "Our horses are weary and need rest. This is a peaceful place, and here we are safe. Your dream was idle fancy, no more."·

We forgot Lone Bird's warning and Wah-lit-its's dream. When the hunters came back, it was a happy night. For supper we ate speckled trout and camas roots baked in ashes and the last of the huckleberries we had picked along the way.

Swan Necklace polished his boots and put bear grease on his hair. He fairly glistened. He said kind words about my eagle-feather and goose-quill jacket and the blue-beaded band I wore around my forehead. But he was so full of his part in battle that he could talk of little else.

I was proud of him. To please him I said, "You'll be a chieftain after just one more battle with the Blue Coats."

"They'll come sneaking along again in a few days and I'll kill some more."

Children made ugly masks of the dead soldiers with eyes hanging down on their cheeks and pieces of ear cut off. They dug holes and buried the masks deep and laughed and hummed secret songs that they made up.

Our ponies and mules were tethered above the stream, where they could be watched during the night. Sentries were placed on the crests of the valley but not enough of them. The camp slept well. In the willows frogs croaked their night song. A child screamed and dogs barked. A woman who had been wounded at White Bird moaned. Those were all the sounds I heard before daybreak.

The sky was cold gray when I woke from a troubled sleep and crawled out of the tipi. I had picked up a pot to fill with water for the morning meal when the first shot crossed the stream. It came from a tree close behind me.

Wah-lit-its, wrapped in his long red coat, had gone out to see that the herd was still safely tied up. He marched along the shore with a warrior's step. A second bullet struck him in the back and knocked him down. He was the one who had killed Richard Devine and started the war, and the enemy knew it.

Wah-lit-its crawled to the stream. He was falling in the water when his wife came out of their tipi. She was heavy with the child she would bear him and walked slowly. She caught him in her arms and held him until he gave one long gasp and was dead.

The man who had killed Wah-lit-its stood over her, saying something I could not hear, putting bullets in his smoking gun. The next bullet struck her in the chest. She staggered but made no sound. Somehow she got the gun from him and took careful aim and shot him in the face. Then she sank to the ground and died.

My father lurched from his bed and ran outside. He thrust my baby sister into my arms. The air was filled with shouts and war whoops and the cries of children, cut through by the sound of shooting. Bullets tore through the camp like hailstones. Fires burned along the shore from one tipi to another. Women with children clutching their skirts and babies on their backs ran out of the tipis screaming. My father told them to leave the stream and hide on the hillside in the brush. By this time all the tipis were burning. My mother ran out with her braided hair on fire.

Some of the women tried to hide in the stream, but it was too shallow and their heads stuck out of the water. Soldiers shot at their heads and killed all except a child who was able to crawl along the bottom and grasp some willows along the shore.

Our warriors drove the soldiers back across the stream and through the willows. Then Looking Glass gathered our warriors and scattered them through the bottom between the stream and the far hills. They dug pits, set up carbines, and built rock walls high enough to shoot over and not to be shot at by the soldiers.

Their guns were not new, and their soft bullets got stuck in the barrels and the barrels exploded. They had no food and it was hard to reach the stream without being shot. Yet from the hour Looking Glass put them in the pits, they fought until the gun barrels melted.

At nightfall Chief Joseph went to the dirt pits and counted. He found thirty-one of our people dead and twenty-six badly wounded. Most of the dead and wounded were women, old men, and children. Some had been shot as they slept, still rolled in their blankets. Some had been clubbed by the soldiers when they charged the camp at dawn. We lost twelve warriors. Red Moccasin Tops was dead, killed by a bullet that struck him in the throat. Of the Red Coats, only Swan Necklace lived.

My father could not count the enemy soldiers who were slain and wounded in the hills, but our warriors said that the Blue Coats lay thick upon the ground. Lean Elk, who had joined us only a few suns before, fought valiantly. He led a group that seized the soldiers' cannon, broke it, and pushed it into the swamp. They captured enough bullets to fight many battles. Yet we had taken a loss we dared not suffer another day.

Fighting stopped when the night hawks began to fly. Swan Necklace and I held hands and talked about the day we would be married and live once more in beautiful Wallowa. We watched two girls combing their wet hair. They had spent most of the day in the stream, swimming in the shallows and coming up to breathe.

Then I went to help with the wounded. My mother had been hit as she ran for the stream, her hair in flames. We fought for her life all night there by the water. My father held her in his arms, away from the smoldering camp and the starlit sky, to the world beyond. When she died, my father said, "Will this hatred ever end? It sickens my heart. All men were made by the same Great Spirit Chief. Yet we shoot one another down like animals."

Eleven

WITH SICK HEARTS, we packed in the dark to leave. Four of our best warriors lay dead. Besides Wah-lit-its and Red Moccasin Tops, we had lost Rainbow and Five Wounds. Only a few families were not mourning a lost relative. The Blue Coats were pinned in rifle pits among the trees and could not see our camp. A dozen of our warriors kept them busy fighting so we could get away.

My father was in charge of our escape. He rounded up the horses and we got ready to go. We pulled down the tipis that had not burned and used the poles to make travois for the badly wounded. With my baby sister on my back, I helped put Fair Land, Ollokot's wife, on a travois. She was near death, but Ollokot was still fighting and could not be with her.

Those whose wounds were not dangerous, we tied onto ponies. I helped White Feather onto her horse. She made a face from pain as I boosted her into the saddle. Early in the fighting, a bullet struck her in the shoulder. It knocked her to the ground and made her dizzy. She grabbed at something to pull herself up. It was the boot of a Blue Coat. He smashed his rifle butt into her face. The blow split her lip and broke one of her front teeth. Her lip was swollen and she was no longer pretty, but she would live.

Before we started off, we buried many of our dead. As we wrapped them in soft buffalo robes, we wailed songs of mourning. The sounds pierced the air as our loss pierced our hearts. With each one, we buried some of that person's prized possessions—a flute, a necklace, bracelets of copper wire, an embroidered headband. When I helped bury my beautiful mother, my tears fell hot on her wrappings. With knives we dug shallow graves in little ravines along the riverbank. There we placed our dead and pulled earth over them.

Chief Joseph led the women, children, old men, and the rest of our warriors away from Big Hole. White Bird, who was too old to fight, rode with us. The other chiefs stayed to fight. We left many buffalo robes and much food. Our things were scattered on the ground.

We traveled toward the low, rolling hills, then swung south toward the mountains. As we moved away, the sounds of battle grew faint. In the gray dawn, a broad path stretched behind us where our ponies' feet trampled the grass. The travois poles made furrows in the ground. Our warriors would find it easy to follow.

The morning mists cleared and the summer sun beat down upon us. Clouds of dust rose around the travois. We stopped often to shade the eyes of our wounded and to wet their parched lips. After a long half-sun, we halted at a little stream shaded by willows. The sun was still in the sky, but our wounded could travel no farther.

That night Fair Land died. My father held her hand as she died and he grieved with me. We grieved for my mother, too. As the spirit of Ollokot's wife entered the afterworld, we saw my mother die again.

My father sighed deeply. "We never make war on women and children," he said. "But the Blue Coats kill our women and children first. That is a shameful way to fight."

The war no longer stirred me. Before this we had beaten the Blue Coats with little trouble. Few of our people had been killed. But now we lost many. My heart was wrenched out of me. I feared for Swan Necklace and I feared for my people.

But I could not think about my fears. Bending Willow cried for my mother and for my mother's milk. I fed her soft mush but she spat it out and cried harder. Then Deer Woman knelt by my side. Her baby had been killed by the Blue Coats. She picked up Bending Willow and held her close, letting her drink the milk that her own baby no longer needed.

We slept little that night. There were many wounded to care for. I carried water, changed bandages, and fed camas mush to those who could eat. I comforted those who cried out in pain.

In the morning, as we were packing the horses, the warriors rode into camp. Swan Necklace was safe.

"Do not fear for me," he said. "Bullets cannot kill me as long as I have my war whistle."

When he went into battle, he sounded his war whistle. It was made from the wing bone of a crane and its piercing cry called Swan Necklace's guardian spirit to protect him.

"Red Moccasin Tops lies dead," I answered.

"His guardian spirit protected him only from wounds on his body," said Swan Necklace. "He was shot in the throat."

"And Wah-lit-its? And Rainbow? And all our other brave warriors who lie dead?"

"Perhaps Wah-lit-its was shot before he could pick up his charm of weasel skin and raven feathers," said Swan Necklace. "Rainbow's guardian spirit protected him in battle only after sunrise. Then he could walk among his enemies. He was struck while the sky was dark."

I wondered at his words and prayed to the Great Spirit Chief to protect him.

We buried Fair Land with her elk-hide dress that she wore on feast days and a shell necklace from the Land of the Great Waters. We wailed songs of grief for her.

Before we left our camp, the War Council met once more. Looking Glass was in disgrace. He had failed the people.

"We have traveled too slowly and have been too careless," said White Bird. "We cannot fight again. If we kill one soldier, a thousand will take his place. But if we lose one warrior, there is no one to take his place."

The council heard his words and chose a new leader. It was Lean Elk, a young warrior with a tight mouth and burning eyes. At noon he sent us south with his burning gaze.

Twelve

LEAN ELK kept us on the move. Warriors rode at the head of our band and in the rear. The women, children, and old men rode in the middle with our extra horses. We were on our ponies before daybreak and traveled until the sun was halfway up the sky. Then we stopped to cook a meal. The ponies grazed while we rested. Then we got back into the saddle and traveled again until long after dark. Each sun we journeyed far.

More of our wounded died. Gray Eagle, the father of White Feather, died after three suns. One old woman who had been hit in the belly stayed behind to die alone. She said she could go no farther on a travois. I believe that she felt she slowed our march and endangered the tribe. We laid her in the shade of a willow and left food and a bottle of water beside her.

We crossed the mountains and turned again toward the rising sun. When we rested, we talked. People talked against the whites and agreed that they were all enemies. Settlers from the Bitterroot Valley had fought beside the soldiers at Big Hole. The same people who had smiled at us and sold us sugar had killed our women and children as they slept. Anger ran deep through the camp.

When our scouts stole horses from the ranches we passed, no Ne-mee-poo said a word against them. The horses we took could not be used by the soldiers who came after us. On one raid for horses, the warriors killed three men on a ranch. But our warriors obeyed Chief Joseph. They did not scalp the dead men. Instead they covered the bodies with blankets. They took no money, only cloth to bandage our wounded.

One morning scouts warned that soldiers were nearby. The one-armed general and his men were at the place we had camped last night, between two clear streams filled with trout. There was shade from cottonwoods and willows and deep grass for horses. The soldiers stopped there to rest.

The chiefs called the warriors together. "If the general has no horses, the Blue Coats cannot ride," said Lean Elk.

"If he has no mules, the general will have no wagons. Without wagons, he cannot follow us. Tonight we steal his herds."

That day we rested in the Camas Meadows. The

camas blossoms had faded. The roots were still small, but we gathered enough to feed us for many suns. Some we ate raw; the rest we dried. We would mix them with huckleberries and shape them into cakes. The cakes were easy to carry on our horses.

While we worked, the chiefs planned the raid. After the sun had dropped behind the mountains, the warriors went out in three bands, with Ollokot, Looking Glass, and Too-hul-hul-sote as leaders. Swan Necklace and Two Moons rode with Ollokot.

When the raiding party left, I slipped out and climbed on my pony. I did not tell my father. I knew he would forbid me to go.

Beneath a half-moon the warriors rode, swift and silent in the night. I rode behind them, careful to stay back so they would not hear me. As we neared the soldiers' camp, the horses slowed.

I watched as the warriors rode among the tethered animals and cut their hobbles. They had worked for only a few minutes when a soldier called, "Who are you there?"

A shot rang out. One of our warriors had fired his gun. It alarmed the soldiers. They began shouting. A bugle sounded.

The warriors yelled and waved buffalo robes to make the herds run. Then they pulled back, firing over their shoulders as they rode away. Before they left, one of the warriors grabbed a blazing stick from a fire and set the wagons ablaze. General Howard was left with piles of ashes.

Suddenly there were wild screams and a herd rushed past, plunging through the mist. Ollokot caught the animals with his fast riders and turned them back toward our camp.

Stampeding animals were all around me. The Great Spirit Chief must have been watching, because the animals parted and made a river on each side of me. I could feel their hot breath, but as they pounded past, they did not even brush my legs.

Swan Necklace rode by with several horses. He did not see me. After he had passed, he fired his rifle and snapped a whip over their backs. The horses screamed and ran in among the herd.

A powerful hand grabbed my arm, the fingers pressing so hard against the bone that I winced. A cold knife blade touched my throat. A gruff voice said, "Who is here?" It was Too-hul-hul-sote.

"It's Sound of Running Feet," I whispered. My mouth was dry with fear.

"Ahhh," he said in disgust. "You are going to get yourself killed." He dropped my arm and put the knife back in his belt. Too-hul-hul-sote snatched my pony's reins, then rode off after the stampeding herd, dragging me behind him.

Before we had ridden far the darkness faded. In the

first gray light, we saw that we had captured only three horses; but we had taken all of the general's mules.

We had no time to talk about the raid. The soldiers were close behind us. Half of the warriors slid off their horses and made ready to fight. The rest of us rode on with the mules.

Too-hul-hul-sote dropped the reins of my pony and slapped it on the rear. "Get back to camp," he shouted, and turned to join the warriors who crouched behind rocks.

Not long after we had reached Camas Meadows, the rest of the warriors came riding in. They were in high spirits. Only one had been struck and his wound was light. The bullet had skimmed his arm. It left a bloody path but did not stop him from joining in the feast. His hurt was so small that the warriors gave him a new name: Little Wound.

It was the happiest time for us. Our warriors sang and old people crooned songs they had forgotten. We had taken a small revenge against the one-armed general. It gave him shame.

A new spirit ran through the camp, some of the same spirit we had before the white general came. We had beaten his soldiers in the battles for the Clearwater and White Bird Canyon.

"We beat them again," Ferocious Bear said.

He sat on his spotted pony and shouted to everyone in the camp, to the lame and to the women who could only weave baskets and gather camas root.

At last he went to our last Red Coat and put a heavy hand on him. He said nothing, just gave Swan Necklace's arm a powerful squeeze.

Thirteen

WE RESTED for a whole sun after the battle. We knew the soldiers could not follow until they got more mules. Lean Elk was less happy than the rest of the camp. He thought we should have taken the horses, too. He called me to his tipi.

I combed my hair and braided it with strips of soft otter skin. I scrubbed my face with a wet cloth. I wiped the dirt off my elk-hide dress. Then I walked slowly across the camp, my skirt brushing the long grass. I was sure I was in trouble.

For a long time Lean Elk was silent. He looked at me with his burning eyes until I felt no bigger than a chipmunk. "I hear you played at warrior last night," he said. He was not pleased.

My words clattered like pebbles. "I . . . I . . . I . . . I . . . w . . . wanted to see the raid," I said.

"And your childish wish cost us a herd of horses," he said.

Anger chased away my fear. "I am not the one who fired the rifle," I said. "I went without a weapon. I am not a warrior, but I am not such a child as to warn the soldiers."

Lean Elk tried to look stern, but the corners of his mouth would not stay still. He drew a hand across his lips to hide his smile. "So you think you know more about war than our brave warriors," he said.

"No," I said. "But I did not fight. I only watched."

"Next time obey your father," he said. "Ne-mee-poo women do not fight."

"The Blue Coats killed my mother. I would fight them if they came again," I said. "I would be as brave as the wife of Wah-lit-its. She fought beside her husband."

"She had battle thrust upon her," said Lean Elk. "You sought it out. You got in the way. Too-hul-hul-sote nearly killed you. He was very angry. Let us have no more of this playing at warrior. It does not become the future wife of a Red Coat."

I did not know what to say. I had been in the way and Too-hul-hul-sote had nearly cut my throat. I nodded and spoke no more.

We left the meadow the next morning in a steady rain. The trail grew steep. After two suns we marched into the Land of the Spirit Fountains, where a broad path ran along the riverbank. Elk and black-tailed deer grazed in the distance. It was still summer on the meadow, but leaves were turning scarlet in the high country. The streams ran from bank to bank with green water that would soon turn to ice. The rivers already were crusted with ice. Chokecherries that puckered the tongue rattled dry and bitter on their stems, yet you could hold your breath, shut your eyes, make a face, and suck them down.

This was a wondrous place. I had heard about its pools of churning mud and its fountains that sprayed into the heavens. Soon we came to a small fountain close to the trail where water bubbled out and ran down to the rims. I stood beside the bubbling water and felt something move beneath my feet, cold with the earth's deepest cold. It grew warm and spread out. It rose around my body with the warmth of human breath. There was a great rumbling and from the center of the pool white clouds of water spouted high above my head into a sky turned suddenly blue.

We had stopped for food when there was a great commotion. The scouts came riding in, but they were not alone. White settlers rode with them.

Two of the settlers were women. The one on a gray horse had seen as many snows as my mother. She had eyes the color of an early morning sky, a narrow nose, and a sharp chin. Her hair was the shade of dried grass, which she had twisted on top of her head. She was so strange looking that I felt sorry for her. She wore many long skirts and sat with both legs on the same side of the horse. It seemed a foolish way to ride.

The one on the spotted horse was younger, no older than I. She too sat sideways. Her eyes were green like spring grass. Her hair, the red-gold of a setting sun, had come loose and hung around her shoulders. Her face was dirty. There were twigs and burrs in her hair and mud on her skirt. I guessed that she had tried to run away.

The women seemed frightened but they stared straight ahead and said nothing.

Chief Joseph walked over and put his hand on the bridle of the gray horse. "Do not be afraid," he said, using white words. "The soldiers killed many of our women and children at Big Hole. But we do not kill women."

The chiefs met in council and decided to let the settlers go, even the men. Lean Elk told them to get off their horses.

When the settlers stood on the ground, a warrior led their fresh horses away. He brought back some of our worn-out ponies. With broken-down horses, it would take them several suns to get to the white soldiers. By then we would be far across the mountains.

"You are free to go," said Lean Elk. "But do not spy on us."

The settlers left quickly. They were glad to get away.

A moon showed in the east beyond the towering peaks of the Absarokas when we saw the settlers again. Fires burned around the edge of our camp. Swan Necklace and Ferocious Bear rode between the fires, pushing one white man and the two women before them.

My father strode over and began to talk with the warriors. His voice rose in anger. Swan Necklace and Ferocious Bear turned their horses away, and my father brought the settlers to our fire.

The settlers had broken their word. Once they were out of sight, the men slid to the ground and came back along the river, spying on our camp. Our scouts found them skulking in the brush along the river. There was a fight, and three of the men ran away. Our scouts captured the woman with yellow hair, her young sister, and her brother. But two of the men were shot. That made my father angry because the settlers had given us their guns.

He shook his head. "Swan Necklace has become as foolish as Wah-lit-its," he said. "He will make trouble for us, killing unarmed men."

I motioned to the settlers to sit down. Yellow Hair and Dirty Face were the first white women I had seen so close. I stared at them. They were not pretty but they did not look evil.

The white man smiled at me. I said to myself that he was a wicked man and would kill me if he could.

I looked away and did not smile.

While I prepared our evening meal, Bending Willow began to cry. I did not leave the fire, but her cries stopped. I heard soft murmurs and turned to see Yellow Hair rocking the cradleboard. Soon Bending Willow was fast asleep.

The settlers ate baked camas roots and antelope I cooked on sticks. They did not complain. After our meal the white man said some words in our tongue to Chief Joseph, but my father would not answer. He stared into the glowing coals. His heart was troubled. I knew he was worried about what to do with our prisoners.

After our meal I sat beside the young, green-eyed prisoner. She shrank back against the buffalo robe held up by stakes that protected us from the cold.

I smiled and touching my chest said, "Sound of Running Feet." Then I waited.

She did not say her name. So I touched her cheek and pointed to her chest. "Dirty Face," I said.

She looked wildly from side to side. It was no use; she did not understand.

That night the settlers slept in front of the fire, next to our shelter. I gave them buffalo robes against the cold. Dirty Face pulled her robe around her and began to cry. Yellow Hair spoke softly to her. She put her arm about the girl's shoulders and comforted her, as a mother would comfort a hurt child. It puzzled me to see that white women acted no different from women of the Ne-mee-poo.

Fourteen

THE NEXT DAY Yellow Hair and her sister rode beside me on two of our ponies. They used our saddles and rode like Ne-mee-poo, with their legs hanging down on each side of the horse. Their full skirts were hiked up over their knees and showed their high boots with many buttons.

A cold wind blew down upon us. Dirty Face's hair whipped around her face, and she kept brushing it out of her eyes. At night she moaned and cried out in her sleep. By day she shrank back in fear each time a warrior passed near her.

There was nothing for her to fear. We did not harm women. I wanted to tell her so, but I had no words to say to Dirty Face and she had no words to say to me. She did not understand my hand signs. A thought came into my head.

I pulled a hat out of my pony's pack. It was a basket hat. Many of our women wore them. I put the hat on. Then I took it off and handed it to her, making signs.

Dirty Face pulled the hat over her flying hair. She smiled a shy smile. She said no words, but for the rest of that day she looked less like a trapped deer.

I felt good inside.

When the shadows grew long, we stopped for the night. Before the ponies were tethered, my father chose two that had carried heavy loads that day. He called to the settlers.

"You go now," he said. "Travel down the river. Go back to your homes."

I gave them bundles of camas-root cakes and dried fish to eat on the way.

Yellow Hair and Dirty Face climbed on the horses. Warriors swam the animals across the river. The white man crossed, riding behind Two Moons. The settlers started off along the riverbank, the man walking beside the horses. With tired ponies and a walking man, they would move slowly. That gave us more time.

For many suns we traveled toward the rising sun. Our path led us past fountains of bubbling mud and beside small lakes. Whenever we could, we followed a stream. Scouts brought word that soldiers waited for us on all the trails. No matter which one we took, the Blue Coats waited for us.

Peaks of the snowy Absaroka Mountains rose up through the falling snow. "There are many tall peaks in the Absarokas," said Lean Elk, "more than the fingers you have on both hands. They all have passages between them, even those that look closed."

He took us through a strange canyon. The towering rocks nearly met over our heads. They shut out the sun and made the world full of dark shadows. No birds sang here and the only sounds came from our ponies' hoofs as they struck the earth and from the roar of the rushing stream below. The path threaded through mountains and between rocks. It twisted and turned. It was so narrow that there was scarcely room for a single horse. In places we could not pass until our scouts had chopped off pine boughs that hung across the path.

Once more we slipped through the general's fingers. We crossed the river on the other side of the Absarokas and entered the land of the Crows.

Looking Glass rode ahead to let the Crows know that our people were on their way. The Crows had always been peaceful with us against the Sioux, the Bannocks, and the cunning Assiniboins.

At last we arrived at a Crow camp. The braves ate with us. They smoked long-stemmed ironwood pipes with the face of their chieftain carved on the bowls and treated us as friends. They gave us bullets. But in the end, fearing the revenge that the White Soldiers might put on them, they refused to help us.

My father called the council—all the chieftains who could give him advice. Lean Elk with his burning gaze, Ollokot, Looking Glass, White Bird, Too-hul-hul-sote, Lone Bird, Yellow Bull, Antelope Red Stone, and Ferocious Bear gathered to talk. Chief Joseph looked at each man as never before.

"Now all the tribes are enemies. Every white man in these mountains is already our enemy," he said. "We were warned on that night, thirteen snows ago, when Preacher Chivington raided Black Kettle's village far south at Sand Creek. With white soldiers he came down on the camp before the sky turned light. He smashed heads, cut throats, slashed off ears. Blood ran across the earth and into the stream. That night the tribes learned to hate the settlers. And now . . ."

"We hate ourselves," said Lean Elk through his teeth.

"Ourselves," shouted young Gray Panther.

Yellow Bull, the father of Red Moccasin Tops, drew a finger across his throat.

Ollokot said nothing.

My father went on. "The one-armed general is far behind us. But the click-clack has told soldiers at every fort to look for us. They come from all sides. We are in danger."

Then Ferocious Bear struggled to his feet and stood silent. From the day we had left Wallowa and crossed the flooding Snake, from the battle of White Bird Canyon, from those days to this moment, no one knew what he thought.

But my father said to the old man in a gentle voice, "Speak."

"Looking Glass has cost us much," said Ferocious Bear. "White Bird said, 'Go north to the Old Lady's country. Go join Sitting Bull.' But we heeded Looking Glass and came south. We have lost many warriors. We have lost many women, many children."

Too-hul-hul-sote nodded his great head. "Ferocious Bear's words are strong," he said. "Looking Glass said the Crows would fight beside us. But the Crows will not help us. They are no longer our brothers. We must travel north to join Sitting Bull."

Looking Glass was angry. His black eyes flashed like his glass when struck by the sun's rays. "So be it," he said.

"So be it," said my father.

Fifteen

FEROCIOUS BEAR and Too-hul-hul-sote were right. In three suns the Blue Coats caught up with us. We were traveling across a broad plain. Our scouts saw the dust from their horses and waved a red blanket to warn us. Lean Elk ordered the warriors to pull their ponies around and get ready to fight. While the warriors waited for the white soldiers, we escaped up a dry streambed into a wide canyon.

For two suns Chief Joseph led us up the canyon. The trail took us across rolling hills covered with sage brush. The canyon rim was rocky and no trees grew there. We saw no Blue Coats, only rabbits and ground squirrels and woodchucks.

The shadows were long when Lean Elk and the warriors joined us. He was angry and at once called the council together. Chief Joseph halted our march and the women made camp while the chiefs met.

Swan Necklace led his pony to our fire. Across its

back lay an antelope. He skinned it and cut the meat into chunks for roasting. We had not had fresh meat since we entered the Absarokas.

"It is a bitter day for us," he said, wiping his knife on a clump of dry grass.

"Were many killed?" I asked.

"None. Three were wounded but not bad." He grinned. "The buffalo gun I took from a ranch shoots good. It speaks so loud the Blue Coats think I have a cannon." For a moment his heart was light.

"The Blue Coats lost many men," he said. "They fight like women."

I was puzzled. "Why was the day bitter?" I asked.

"The Crows fought beside the Blue Coats," he said, his mouth twisting with disgust. "When I saw them my heart was just like fire. We battled the Crows for two suns."

I caught my breath. The world was against us. We could not fight forever.

Swan Necklace saw the fear in my eyes. He placed a gentle hand on my chin and turned my face toward him. "Do not fret, my love," he said. "As long as I live no Blue Coat will harm you."

I smiled with my lips but not with my heart.

He loaded the rest of the antelope onto his pony and took it to the cooking fire of Two Moons.

Before the morning star shone we broke camp.

Lean Elk urged us to hurry. He said we must now fear all the tribes. We must go fast to the Old Lady's country.

We left the canyon and moved north for six suns. Lean Elk drove us from dark to dark. The stars shone above us when we got onto our horses and they shone when we got off. We rested little and traveled much. We were weary and our ponies were weary.

When we struck camp the frost glittered on the prairie like a lake sparkling in the sun. The ground was still hard when the sun climbed halfway up the sky. I no longer packed my buffalo robe. After I climbed on my pony, I pulled it around me and Bending Willow.

Our food ran low. There was no time to hunt. On the morning that we came to a herd of mountain sheep, there were only two cakes of camas roots and berries in the bag on my pony's saddle. The young men killed several sheep but not enough to stay our hunger. Each family got only one small piece of meat. We waited until nightfall to eat it. We did not stop to cook while the sun was high.

We buried the skins and the horns beside the trail. It hurt me to see the fleecy skins covered with earth, but we had no time to tan them for robes or make the horns into drinking cups.

One day we met a band of Crows. They had been

hunting and had camped to dry buffalo meat. They were no longer our brothers, so we took their horses and left our worn-out ponies behind. With fresh horses we could move faster.

On the sixth sun we came to a great river. On the other shore stood a few buildings. Beside them were boxes and boxes filled with supplies for the soldiers. At this place the river was broad but not deep. The water was so low that we could swim our horses across. There was no need to make bullboats.

Some of our warriors crossed the river first. They called us to follow them. There were only a few white men and they did not want to fight.

Our food was almost gone. My father asked the white men for food. They gave him a slab of bacon and a small sack of hard bread. It was so little that it was worthless.

My father's eyes were hard and angry. He led us up a small creek and told us to make camp. Then he left with the warriors. Soon we heard guns speak. The shooting went on until light streaked the eastern sky.

It was not long after that the warriors rode into camp. They called us to bring the pack ponies and follow them. We hurried back to the river.

The white men had fled. The warriors chopped open the boxes and we loaded the horses. We took flour and sugar, beans and bacon. We took coffee. We took pots to cook in—the first we had seen since Big Hole. The camp would feast that night.

After we had loaded the ponies, our warriors burned the rest of the supplies. No Blue Coats would eat that food. As we rode north, a cold wind carried the smell of smoke from the river.

Sixteen

THERE WAS ICE on the ground and the wind blew hard. We suffered from the cold. The people wanted to rest. The old people said their bones were sore from so many days in the saddle. They wanted to rest beside a warm fire. The women said their children needed sleep. Their eyes were hollow and their gaze was dim. There was no joy in the camp.

Lean Elk stopped the march early. Once more the chiefs met. Their voices grew loud.

"We must keep going," said Lean Elk. "When we cross the Bear Paw Mountains we will come to the Old Lady's country. In three suns I will take us to Sitting Bull."

"We are tired," said Looking Glass. "The old cannot travel at this pace. The children weep with weariness. We have beans and flour. We are in buffalo country. If we travel slow, our young men can kill buffalo."

White Bird got to his feet. "Looking Glass speaks foolish words," he said. "Until we leave this country, we are hunted by Blue Coats."

But White Bird was the only chief who sided with Lean Elk.

Chief Joseph looked around the circle. He looked deep into the eyes of the chiefs. He looked into his heart. "I fear for the lives of the old people," he said. "And I fear for us all. If we go fast, our ponies may wear out. Their hoofs are tender and some limp. If we go slow, we may be caught by the Blue Coats."

"Do not worry about the Blue Coats," said Too-hul-hul-sote. His hand cut the air to show his contempt for the soldiers. "They are at least two days behind us. We can travel slow and stay ahead of them."

"Lean Elk is no chief for us," said Looking Glass. He stood tall and proud. His black hat trimmed with otter fur made him loom over the seated chiefs. "A chief does not wear out his people. A chief does not wear out his horses. Lean Elk should lead us no longer."

Lean Elk stared hard at Looking Glass. His eyes were coals of hot fire. "All right, Looking Glass," he said. "You can lead. I am trying to save the people. You take command. But I think we will be caught and killed."

He walked away from the chiefs and stood alone, a

silent figure in the gathering dark. He stared at the distant Bear Paw Mountains.

Looking Glass led us on short marches toward the star that never moves. We started after the sun rose and stopped before it left the sky. The people no longer muttered.

After four suns we crossed the Bear Paw Mountains. We were close to the lands of Sitting Bull. We traveled through a barren valley with no trees. Sagebrush grew here, but the long grass had frozen and was brown. It bent in the cold wind.

We had been riding for a short while when Swan Necklace came back from the trail ahead. He said that the scouts had killed buffalo. The meat waited for us in a cove beside a stream. The sun was overhead when we reached the grasslands where the meat lay. Looking Glass said we would rest here until morning.

Lean Elk said that we must keep on. This was a bad place to camp. Soldiers could sweep down on us from either side. But Looking Glass said our horses needed more rest. We would stay.

He had chosen a cold place. The wind from the Old Lady's country swept across the land, turning our bones to ice. We had no tipis because we had left all our poles at Big Hole. The children huddled in deep ravines beside the creek while we made shelters with buffalo skins and canvas.

There was no wood but many buffalo chips lay on the ground. They burned well. Soon fires blazed across the camp. We ate roasted buffalo until we could hold no more.

Around the warm fires people said what a good leader Looking Glass was. In less than two suns we would be safe with Sitting Bull. Looking Glass had been right to march slow.

It was a clear cold night. The wind blew hard and the brush stirred along the creek. Many chose to spend the night in the gullies, which were as deep as a standing man.

Swan Necklace walked with me beside the creek. Buffalo robes wrapped us together against the cold. His arm was around my shoulder.

"Do not look so sad," he said. "Soon we will be safe. Then my father will let the marriage go forward."

"When you finish our marriage blanket," I said. It seemed strange to be talking about something besides the Blue Coats behind us.

"That will be soon," he said. He pressed me to him. "I will gather colored earth from the Old Lady's land. It will be a beautiful blanket. We will sleep beneath it in our own tipi."

The words were like honey to my ears, yet I was not at peace. I feared that Lean Elk was right.

A misshapen moon streaked with red rode low in the eastern sky. I wondered if the ugly moon was a warning from the Great Spirit. Was it blood I saw on the rising moon?

That night I lay awake worrying about the soldiers. I heard the ponies moving about. They were restless. I was restless, too. I trembled at the thought of what the morning might bring.

Seventeen

THE MORNING AIR was cold with a hint of snow. Clouds gathered in the sky. We began to pack our things. Some people sat by their fires. They chewed on buffalo meat from last night's feast. Bending Willow was in the arms of Deer Woman, having her morning milk. Children played games beside the stream with sticks and balls of mud. We were happy with the thought that in two suns we would be in safe country.

Scouts rode into camp, their braids flying behind them. "Buffalo!" they shouted. "Stampeding buffalo!"

Only one thing would stampede the buffalo: Blue Coats. The soldiers were near. I hurried but my fingers would not obey me. The knots in the rawhide that held the skin shelter remained fast.

"Do not hurry!" said a voice. Looking Glass rode by our shelter. He went from one end of the camp to the other, saying, "Go slow! We have much time."

I slowed down. My fingers began to work again.

A short while later I heard a shriek.

It came from young Joseph, who was across the stream. He pointed at a bluff behind us. There, outlined against the morning sky, sat a warrior on a spotted horse. On his head was a war bonnet of eagle feathers. It was a Cheyenne who scouted for the Blue Coats.

Young Joseph splashed through the icy water. He came out of the stream with his teeth chattering. He had lost his moccasins and wore only a shirt. I wrapped him in a buffalo robe with pushed him into a gulch.

The sound of galloping horses grew loud. All the Blue Coats in the world must have been on the other side of the rise. I looked up to see soldiers riding down upon us, Blue Coats on horses spread out in two wide wings that circled the camp. They were led by Cheyenne scouts.

People were running in every direction.

My father ran toward the herd. "The horses," he called. "Save the horses."

Warriors grabbed their rifles and got into gullies and behind rocks. Hoof beats and gunfire made it hard to hear.

Through the line of Blue Coats stampeded our horses, their eyes wild, their manes streaming. My father rode with them. He had no gun, no bow. There were white soldiers on every side of him. I held my breath. With a burst of speed he reached us and jumped from his horse. Blood coursed down the side of his horse, but it was not the blood of my father. His guardian spirit rode with him.

Chief Joseph caught a pony as it raced by. Handing me the reins, he said, "Flee, daughter. Ride to the north. Go to Sitting Bull."

He ran to help others.

I stood with the reins in my hand. Bullets flew around me. I looked for Deer Woman, but she was not there. I looked into the gully. Young Joseph crouched at the bottom. Beside him knelt a women who was great with child.

I motioned for them to climb out. "Here," I said. "Ride for Sitting Bull. Now!"

Young Joseph pushed the woman on the horse and climbed up behind her. I slapped the pony and it bolted off.

I saw many people grabbing horses and riding away. A woman rode by on a gray horse. A Cheyenne rode up, hoofs pounding, and grabbed her bridle. He fired his pistol. The bullet struck her in the back and she fell to the ground.

Caught in a rain of bullets, horses screamed and died. I looked around for another pony, but the horses had gone. I was trapped.

I leaped into the gully. Bullets passed over my

head. I could not look out. I hoped that Bending Willow and Deer Woman were safe.

I heard war cries and gunfire above me. The war whoops of our warriors mingled with the shouts of the white soldiers. Then the fighting moved away.

A warrior rolled over the edge and into the gully beside me. He landed heavily in the dirt. It was Swan Necklace. Blood covered his left arm. He had a gun in each hand.

"Keep them loaded," he said. He tossed me one of the guns and a pouch of bullets. "We have pushed the Blue Coats out of our camp. Now we will fight to the death."

All that day we fought pinned in the gully. The Blue Coats fired at us from behind rocks. Some shot from behind their dead horses. We were too busy to talk but our eyes spoke for us.

When the shadows fell, the firing died away. Now and again a lone rifle barked. Without the sun the air grew even colder. Some of us were wrapped in robes, but like Swan Necklace, our warriors were stripped for battle. They fought without leggings. They had no shirts and most had no moccasins. Wearing only breechcloths, they shivered in the cold.

Snow fell silently over the land. In the gathering darkness I peered over the edge of the gully and saw bodies strewn across the plain. Children cried with cold and fear and pain.

People began to crawl across the ground, keeping flat so the soldiers would not see them. Warriors came in from the rocks and hollows. They brought news. The news was not good.

Many were dead. Three of our dead were women, and the rest were warriors. Some of our greatest warriors would fight no more. Brave Ollokot, my uncle, was dead. He had fought from behind a rock, where he had killed many Blue Coats. But when he rose to fire his rifle, he was struck in the forehead. Too-hul-hul sote was dead. His body lay on the field in front of the Blue Coats, where we could not retrieve it. Lone Bird was dead. Lean Elk was dead. These last two deaths were bitter, because the bullets that killed them did not come from the Blue Coats but from our own warriors who mistook them for Cheyenne scouts.

We buried our dead, those we could reach. As we did at Big Hole, we dug shallow graves in the sides of the gullies. There was no time for a proper burial. We shoved them into the holes and covered them with earth.

We had plenty of buffalo chips but did not start fires. The light would give the Blue Coats an easy target. We shared cold buffalo and cakes of camas root. I did not eat, nor did most of the other women. We gave the food to the children first, then to the warriors.

We had gone all day without water. Two by two,

we crawled to the stream. We tied buffalo horn cups to rawhide and let them down into the water. When it was my turn I gulped the icy water. It was sweeter than honey to my dry throat.

No one slept that night. With camas hooks and knives we dug deep trenches to shelter our people. Above the trenches, on the low bluffs, we dug shallow rifle pits for the warriors. We used pans to throw the dirt out of the holes we dug. As I dug with my camas hook I wondered if we would ever be safe.

Eighteen

MORNING CAME but the sun hid its face. The cold wind was thick with falling snow. Between our camp and the soldiers the snow was so deep that I could not make out the bodies that littered the frozen ground.

With first light the shooting began. Soon the air was filled with smoke from rifles and I could no longer see the falling snowflakes. Through the mist I saw flashes of guns.

That day while the warriors fought, we dug tunnels in the damp earth with our knives and camas hooks. By nightfall we could scoot on our stomachs from one sheltering gully to the next.

I crept through the tunnels until I found Deer Woman. She and Bending Willow were safe. I swept Bending Willow in my arms and held her close. She waved her small fists and gurgled with laughter. My sister had been on this earth for four moons. I thought that she might not live to see another moon.

97

I gave Deer Woman the buffalo meat I had not eaten. She needed food to make milk for my sister.

That night I stayed in the gully with Deer Woman and Bending Willow. We sat with our backs against the dirt wall. Our hearts were heavy and we talked little.

I slept briefly, but mostly I thought of our beautiful valley, of its blue lake and its wandering streams, its mountain peaks and sheltering valleys, its tall trees and green meadows. I thought I would never see it again.

When the sky grew light the battle began anew. By now those who could escape had reached Sitting Bull. Word passed through the tunnels that he would surely send a war party of Sioux to help us. If help did not come soon, we would be beaten. Our warriors were careful to shoot only when they saw a careless Blue Coat, but our bullets would not last forever.

The rifle fire from the soldiers died away. It became a war of sharpshooters. But the soldiers' big cannon spoke all day. It threw bursting shells into the air. Pieces of metal rained down on us and we held buffalo hides above our heads to keep them off.

Some time after midday the soldiers stopped firing the cannon. A great quiet spread over the plain.

I heard shouts and climbed onto a heap of buffalo skins so I could look over the edge of the gully. The snow had stopped and I could see across the plain. My heart caught in my throat. A white flag waved above the camp of the Blue Coats. It was the sign for truce.

A voice called, "Colonel Miles wants to see Joseph."

My father did not trust the soldiers. He sent Tom Hill, a Ne-mee-poo who could speak the white man's words, to talk with the Blue Coats.

Before the sun had crept the width of a lodge pole, Tom Hill called for my father. The colonel would meet Joseph in the space between the two camps.

My father left his rifle pit. With two warriors he walked toward the soldiers' camp. Several Blue Coats walked toward him. General Howard was not with them. One of the officers had silver birds on his shoulder. It was Colonel Miles. Tom Hill walked beside him.

They met in the center of the plain. Chief Joseph laid down his rifle. The warriors placed their rifles on the ground. For a time they talked to the Blue Coats. The colonel waved his arms and pointed at our camp and then behind him. My father shook his head and made the hand sign that means "never."

He turned and began walking back to his rifle pit. The white colonel pulled a pistol from his belt. The other Blue Coats grabbed my father and held his arms in back of him. They shoved him around and marched him back to the soldiers' camp.

Anger rose in my throat. Again the Blue Coats had broken a truce. My father trusted too much, and now he was a prisoner.

Then something strange happened. A white officer rode into our camp. It was a curious thing for him to do.

Yellow Bull acted quickly. As the officer passed him, Yellow Bull grabbed the reins with one hand and pulled the Blue Coat from his horse with the other. Our warriors surrounded the officer and pushed him into the gully where I stood.

The warriors jumped down after him.

"Kill him!" shouted Two Moons. He pulled a knife from his belt and took one step toward the officer.

"Yes, kill the soldier who wars on women and children," said Swan Necklace.

"Kill the soldier who shames the flag of truce," said Ferocious Bear.

The warriors moved closer to the officer. His back was pressed against the wall of earth, but he did not drop his eyes. He looked at Two Moons and his gaze was steady.

Yellow Bull stepped between them. "Wait," he said.

White Bird came through the tunnel. He stood and stretched out his hand. "You are children," he said. "Do not harm this man. As long as he lives, Joseph is safe. When he dies, the Blue Coats will kill Joseph."

Tom Hill, who was back among us, came in from one of the rifle pits. He talked long with the officer and changed his words so we could understand.

The officer's name was Lieutenant Jerome. He had come to see if we were ready to surrender.

White Bird laughed, but it was a dry sound without joy. "This Blue Coat is also a child," he said. "Let him stay in this shelter. Yellow Bull will guard him. Sound of Running Feet will see that he has water and food and a buffalo robe to keep him warm. Those are my words."

The old chief left through the tunnel and worked his way back to the rifle pits. Two Moons beckoned to Swan Necklace and crawled into the tunnel. Before leaving, Swan Necklace turned toward me and put his hand over his heart in the sign of love.

The soldier spent the night wrapped warmly in a buffalo robe. He slept soundly, but Yellow Bull and I did not sleep at all.

When the soldier awoke he washed his hands and face in water that I brought from the stream. He drank two buffalo horns filled with water and ate buffalo meat and cold mush while Yellow Bull and I watched. He walked back and forth, back and forth. Yellow Bull's eyes followed him. He sat with his rifle across his knees. The soldier had no chance to escape, but he showed no fear.

The soldier Jerome pulled a piece of white paper from his pocket. He took out a pencil and made many marks on the paper. Then he called for Tom Hill.

When Tom Hill came into the shelter, the soldier

spoke the marks. Tom Hill told us what the marks said. They said that the soldier had good food, a warm bed, and good treatment. He hoped that the Blue Coats were treating Chief Joseph the same way.

White Bird sent Tom Hill to the Blue Coats with the talking paper. Soon Tom Hill was back with a talking paper for the soldier. It said that the white colonel would send my father back to us if we would let the soldier Jerome go free.

"No," said White Bird. "The Blue Coats have tricked us before. They will not trick us again. If the colonel speaks true, he will bring Joseph to the ground where we met before. We will bring the soldier Jerome to the same ground."

Tom Hill put these words so the soldier could understand. He changed them into marks on the paper, and Tom Hill carried it back to the white colonel.

He watched Tom Hill enter the camp of the Blue Coats. We waited. Soon my father walked onto the plain. White officers were on each side of him.

Yellow Bull told the soldier Jerome to climb out of the gully. White Bird and Looking Glass waited for him. Two Moons and Ferocious Bear joined them. All walked out to meet the Blue Coats.

The soldier Jerome shook hands with my father. They changed places. Our chiefs and warriors brought my father back to our camp. The Blue Coats pulled down their white flag and the shooting began.

Nineteen

OUR WARRIORS FOUGHT the rest of that day and
the next. They fought with new anger. Chief Joseph
had not been treated as an honored prisoner. The Blue
Coats tied his hands behind him, then tied his hands
to his feet. They rolled him in a blanket like a pa-
poose. He could not stand. He could not walk. He
could not use his arms. The white soldiers slept in a
tent, but my father lay all night beside the mules,
without food or water. He was not untied until the
paper that speaks came from the soldier Jerome.

Two suns came and went. We had lost no people since the first day of battle, but food was short.
Soon even the children would have to go hungry. We
were cold and wet with snow. The cruel wind cut
to our very bones. The children cried. The women
and old men said nothing, but there was pain in their
eyes.

The third sun was a sad time for us. The sadness

began in the morning when it grew light and we saw that a party of white soldiers had arrived during the darkness. The one-armed general had joined Colonel Miles. An army of Blue Coats would soon spread across the land.

When the shooting began that morning, the first shells fell among us. During the night the white soldiers had dug a trench for their cannon and the shells no longer struck the bluffs beyond the rifle pits.

Another act of shame. The soldier Jerome knew that no warriors were in the shelter pits. Again they warred on the helpless.

Shells fell among the women and the children, the old men and the wounded warriors. One shell burst in a shelter pit, covering six of our people with earth. We dug fast, scooping away the choking dirt with pots and hats and our hands.

I pulled a small boy from the pit. His eyes and ears and mouth were full of earth and he gasped for air, but he was safe. Others dragged three women to safety. But we could not reach an old woman and her granddaughter. There was too much dirt. Without air, they died.

My father said that we were beaten. The time had come to surrender.

Not everyone agreed. Some of the warriors wanted to charge the Blue Coats. They said the Blue Coats were bad fighters. We might whip them and be free to join Sitting Bull. They would be glad to die for the people.

My father said no. We could not fight the cannon, and there were too many soldiers. All our warriors would die, and the women and children and old men would be at the mercy of the Blue Coats. My father reminded them of what had happened to the women and children at Big Hole. It was better to return to Lapwai and live on the reservation.

Looking Glass said he would never surrender. He looked at my father. "I am older than you," he said. "I know the white generals are men with two faces and two tongues. If you surrender, you will be sorry. It is better to be dead."

White Bird held up his hand. "Looking Glass speaks the truth," he said. "Surrender if you wish. We will not stop you. We will take those who would rather die and strike out for the Old Lady's country."

The council broke up. The sadness was not yet over. A rider on horseback appeared in the distance. Looking Glass believed it was a Sioux scout, part of a band from Sitting Bull. He stepped out of his rifle pit for a close look. A bullet struck him in the head and he fell sprawled and silent on the ground.

We had lost another chief. Now only my father and White Bird were left to lead us. My father was not a war chief and White Bird was old.

Under a white flag, my father crossed the plain to

the camp of the Blue Coats. The day was gray and he was wrapped in a gray blanket. His head was down. His rifle lay across the saddle. Wearily, he climbed from his horse and walked up to Colonel Miles.

"Let us stop fighting," said Colonel Miles. "No more battles, no more blood."

The one-armed general stood beside him. Ice crystals clung to his beard. "The war is over," he said. "I have lost brothers. Many of you have lost brothers. Do not worry more. It is time for us to rest."

Even with his head bowed, my father towered over General Howard. He drew his blanket closer about him and nodded but did not speak.

Colonel Miles said that he had plenty of food and warm blankets for us. He promised that he would take our people to a nearby camp for the winter. Then we could all go back to our old homes.

The one-armed general watched Chief Joseph and Colonel Miles shake hands. Then my father walked back to his pony and picked up his rifle.

General Howard reached for it.

Chief Joseph pulled back the hand holding the gun. He stood very tall. He looked down at the one-armed general. "I am not surrendering to you," he said. He pointed to Colonel Miles. "This is the man that ran me down."

My father turned to Colonel Miles. He handed him his gun, butt first. Then he stepped back.

"I am tired of fighting," he said. "Our chiefs are killed. Looking Glass is dead. The old men are all killed. He who led the young men is dead. It is cold and we have no blankets. The little children are freezing to death. My people, some of them, have run away to the hills, and have no blankets, no food. No one knows where they are, perhaps freezing to death. I want time to look for my children and see how many of them I can find. Maybe I shall find them among the dead."

He raised his arm. His blanket flapped in the raw wind. "Hear me, my chiefs," he called. "I am tired. My heart is sick and sad. From where the sun now stands, I will fight no more forever." In sorrow, he drew his blanket over his head.

One by one, our warriors stepped from the rifle pits and filed across the plain. They laid their rifles on the ground in front of the generals.

From the shelter pits came the women and children, followed by the old. Wounded warriors crawled from the pits. Some of them leaned on the women and old men. Some of them crawled on their hands and knees. Slowly, the long lines of people moved across the ground and up the hill.

My heart was filled with sadness. I could not join them. Even when I saw Deer Woman trudge slowly up the hill bearing Bending Willow on her back, I could not join them.

Twenty

THE LIGHT FADED and darkness came as I crouched in the gully. The Blue Coats bandaged the wounds of our warriors and let the people bury our dead. They passed out food and blankets. Smoke rose from cooking fires.

The smell of food filled my mouth with water. I had not eaten for three days. Hungry and cold and sad, I huddled against the dirt wall and shut my eyes.

While my father spoke to the generals, White Bird and a large band of our people had slipped away from the camp and started north. Now they were a long march away.

I must start alone for the Old Lady's country, I told myself. But I would wait until the camp was asleep.

As the night wore on, voices died away. Soon all was quiet. A horse nickered, a man coughed, a baby cried. Nothing more. Still I waited.

I waited until the stars moved the space of my two hands across the heavens. Then I wrapped a pan, a knife, and a buffalo horn for water in my wedding blanket. I crawled to the end of the gully that was farthest from the camp.

As I crept over the dirt, my hand touched something hard and cold. I ran my fingers over the object. It was a rifle. I stuck the barrel through the knot on my bundle and pulled myself out of the gully.

The glow of watch fires outlined the edge of the camp. I crawled to the creek, squeezed through the brush, and let myself over the side. Silent as a snake in a stream, I slid down the bank to the water.

Before I could get up, a strong hand clamped over my mouth. Another hand grabbed my arm. "Quiet!" whispered a rough voice.

Fear struck through me. I did not move.

The hands relaxed their grip. "Are you not going home with Chief Joseph?" asked the voice, gentler now.

I peered through the darkness. It was Swan Necklace. He had not surrendered with the warriors. A burst of joy rose in me.

"I am going to Sitting Bull," I said. "I will never go with the white man."

"Let us start," said Swan Necklace. "Better we die together than trust ourselves to those who speak with two tongues."

We followed the creek until it turned back toward the camp. Then we climbed out of the gully and began to walk toward the star that never moves.

Snow covered the ground. Swan Necklace was still stripped for battle. He had no moccasins. I untied my bundle and cut strips of buffalo hide from the robe. Swan Necklace wrapped his feet in the soft fur and pulled our wedding blanket around his shoulders. He carried our guns and I carried the rest.

We walked until light streaked the sky. My moccasins were worn and my feet ached with cold. Swan Necklace said nothing but his legs were bare.

Swan Necklace found us a protected place out of the wind. While he dug a hollow on the side of the hill, I looked for buffalo chips. They were covered with snow and hard to spot, but I found enough for a small fire.

We rubbed each other's feet to warm them, then huddled beneath the blanket. Heat from the fire spread through us and we slept until the sun was high.

I woke to the touch of Swan Necklace's fingers. He brushed my cheek until my eyes opened. "Wake, my love," he said softly. "We must be on our way."

It was our first good sleep since our people came through the Bear Paws. I scrubbed my face with snow to waken me. We had no food. I cut the elk-hide fringe from my skirt and we chewed the strips as we walked. It fooled our stomachs for a time.

The going was hard. Cold wind blew down from the Old Lady's country. We had to push hard against it. Its icy fingers poked under our robes and made us shiver.

It was almost dusk when Swan Necklace spotted an antelope searching for grass in the snow. He aimed carefully. The shot echoed through the quiet air and the antelope fell dead.

We ran to where it lay, its blood making a scarlet pool on the snow. Swan Necklace knelt and began to skin the antelope. I pulled out my knife to help him.

Suddenly a hunting party rode over the hill. They galloped toward us. The snow muffled the sound of the horses' hoofs, but the jingle of their bridles sounded loud in my ears. I knew by their rawhide saddles that they were Assiniboins.

My heart beat like a woodpecker pounding on a lodge pole. The Assiniboins were a fierce tribe and made many wars. They had never been our friends. Were they helping the Blue Coats as the Cheyennes and the Crows and the Flatheads had done?

The horses stopped beside us. There were five riders and five extra horses. They had been on a long hunt, and two of the horses carried meat and hides.

Their leader raised his arm in greeting. He had

been on this earth as many snows as my father. Strips of ermine showed white in his braids. His beaded moccasins were made of soft elkskin. Beneath his saddle was a fine blanket of red wool and otter skins. It was a chief's blanket. Across his saddle lay an old musket, the kind most of our warriors used before we picked up rifles on the battlefield.

The other four men had no guns. They carried bows made from the horns of mountain sheep. They must have traded with our people for them, because only the Ne-mee-poo made such bows.

The leader made signs to say that all the tribes were brothers. He touched his chest and said his name was Red Elk.

We signed back that we were friends and said our names. We signed that we were fleeing from the Blue Coats and on the way to join Sitting Bull.

Red Elk nodded. He spoke a few words of our language. With signs and words he told us that the hunting party was on its way to a nearby Assiniboin village. We were welcome to join them.

His words were good but I did not trust him. When Red Elk saw our fine rifles that had once belonged to white soldiers, his eyes gleamed. His eyes followed them as we put them across our saddles. His eyes stayed on them all the way to the Assiniboin village.

Twenty-one

RED ELK RODE into the village. Tipis clustered near a stream and fires burned bright beside them. A vast herd of ponies was tethered beyond the tipis. Women, children, and old men shouted greetings. They came to look at the load of meat and they came to look at us. They stared hard.

A child poked Swan Necklace's foot wrappings with a curious finger. A woman touched my elkskin skirt. The leather was white as snow and it had taken many suns to sew on the blue quills. She rubbed the skirt between her fingers, then frowned when she saw the ragged edges. I was glad that I had cut away the fringe to stay our hunger. It saved my skirt.

Red Elk motioned to Swan Necklace and me. We got off the horses and followed him to his tipi. Children pointed at us as we walked through the village. Dogs barked. I wondered what the Assiniboin would do with us.

At Red Elk's tipi, Alighting Dove, his wife, was cooking. She was a small woman and moved quickly, like a bird. She speared a chunk of antelope meat and placed it over the fire. In a large pot, kouse mush bubbled. The good smell made me feel weak.

Swan Necklace ate with Red Elk and Charging Hawk, his son. Alighting Dove and I brought them food.

Charging Hawk was a young warrior. He had more snows than Swan Necklace but he did not have a wife. He was short and thick through the chest. Pieces of shell from the Land of the Great Waters gleamed green and blue and silver in his braids. He wore fringed leggings and a buckskin shirt trimmed with elk's teeth. On each arm were many copper bracelets.

Red Elk told Swan Necklace that we were a long day's walk from the Old Lady's country. If we started before the first sun, we would be there in darkness. Swan Necklace nodded. He used signs to tell Red Elk about the surrender and Red Elk said he had seen our people begin a long march toward the rising sun.

After the men had eaten, Alighting Dove and I made our meal. My hunger was so great that I ate with unseemly haste. I saw her watching me and ducked my head with shame. Then I chewed slowly until my hunger was gone.

Alighting Dove looked at my worn moccasins and pulled a new pair from a pack. I thanked her with signs and she patted me on the shoulder. She seemed kind.

Charging Hawk gave Swan Necklace a pair of moccasins and an old shirt and leggings. When Swan Necklace put them on, the sleeves barely covered his elbows and the leggings ended just below his knees. Red Elk and his son laughed at the sight.

I was beginning to forget my fear and slept well that night in the tent of Red Elk.

The morning sky was streaked with red. We started off before the sun. Alighting Dove gave us a packet of food and Red Elk gave us ten bullets for our rifles.

We had walked only a short way from the village when I heard a footstep behind us. That was all. There was one more step, then a knife flashed and Swan Necklace lay on the ground with a deep gash in his neck.

I turned quickly and saw Charging Hawk wiping the blood from his knife. My rifle was not loaded. Before I could pull the knife from my belt, I felt a noose slip around my neck. It drew tight and the world went black.

I opened my eyes. Above me was the wall of Red Elk's tipi. My ankles were tied together and so were my wrists. I looked around.

Alighting Dove sat next to the opening. She was sewing red and blue beads on a moccasin.

I shut my eyes and pretended I was not awake. I

thought hard. I remembered the look in Red Elk's eyes when he saw our rifles. I knew Swan Necklace was dead. I wondered why I still lived, but I did not care. It made no difference now if they killed me.

The shadows were long when Alighting Dove shook me. I looked at her with eyes of hate but said nothing.

She untied my ankles and wrists and led me down to the stream. I could not run away because she held fast to the rawhide around my arm.

When I was ready to leave, she touched me over my heart and touched her eyes and then her heart. She signed that she felt my grief. Her fingers were gentle and so were her eyes.

Tears spilled out of my eyes and ran down my cheeks. I could not speak.

Alighting Dove led me to the place where Swan Necklace lay dead. She signed that I might bury him. I wrapped my love in our wedding blanket. On his chest I placed his war whistle, which had protected him in battle but did not save him from death. I laid him in a shallow grave and chanted a song of mourning. The death of Swan Necklace had taken my heart away. In my breast where my heart once beat was a piece of cold stone.

Twenty-two

FOR SEVEN SUNS I stayed in the tipi of Red Elk. I was not permitted to go outside unless Alighting Dove held the rawhide lead. At night I was tethered to a tipi pole like a horse.

The rifles that Red Elk had taken from us were always before my eyes. He wrapped the barrels in antelope hide and placed them against the wall of the tipi. All day I looked at them and all day I thought of the treachery that had led to the death of Swan Necklace.

At first I did not know why my life was spared. Red Elk paid no attention to me. He looked through me and never spoke. Alighting Dove was kind but never asked me to work. Yet a captive woman is not allowed to be idle.

I listened to their talk. After a few suns some of their words had meaning. I did not let them know how many Assiniboin words I had learned.

From their talk at night I discovered that Charging Hawk once had a wife. She had died three snows before. She was big with child and her baby died with her. For three snows Charging Hawk had grieved and looked at no other woman, even though Red Elk urged him to take a new wife.

Now Charging Hawk had plans for me. He found me more pleasing than any of the Assiniboin women.

Their words told me why Charging Hawk spent much time in the tipi, something warriors did not do in good weather. He sat on the side making arrows and watching me out of the corner of his eye. If I stared at him, he grinned foolishly.

Soon Charging Hawk had filled a quiver with arrows, each one as long as his arm to the tips of his fingers. I could tell they were not war arrows, because they had narrow blades so that they could be pulled out of the animal's flesh and used again. Arrows meant for battle had short, broad tips, with hooks on them so that they stuck tightly and tore the flesh when pulled.

On the seventh sun, Charging Hawk oiled his hair with bear grease and wrapped his braids in otter fur. From his ears hung ornaments of polished metal. He put on his finest clothes. His buckskin shirt was decorated with green porcupine quills. From the shoulder straps hung strands of hair from scalps he had taken.

On the back was painted a red hand, the sign that he had killed another warrior in hand-to-hand combat. At his throat was a necklace of enormous bear claws.

From my seat beside the fire I watched Charging Hawk place a fox skin on a pole some distance away. He walked to a clearing on the other side of the tipi. When he was certain I looked at him, he pulled a handful of arrows from the quiver at his belt. There were as many arrows as fingers on his two hands. Quickly he shot the arrows, his hands moving so fast that they blurred. Before the first had hit the fox skin, the last was moving through the air. All the arrows hit the skin in a spot no larger than my hand.

Without speaking, Charging Hawk plucked the arrows from the pole and marched off. He had shown me his skill as a marksman. I could be certain that those in his tipi would never want for meat.

That night Alighting Dove told me that Charging Hawk wished to marry me. She said that I was lucky. Most captive women became slaves, but as the wife of Charging Hawk I would be an Assiniboin.

Charging Hawk was a great warrior and a skillful hunter, but I felt only hatred for him. Now I must become his wife.

After that day Alighting Dove gave me work to do, but she always worked beside me. She watched me closely and showed me the Assiniboin way to roast roots and dry meat. She showed me how they stored their dried food for winter. She did many things in the Ne-mee-poo way, but some were different.

I learned how to cook meat as the Assiniboins did. Alighting Dove showed me how to dig a hole in the ground and line it with rawhide. She filled the hole with water and put a big chunk of buffalo in it. Into the water she dropped large, red hot stones from the fire. She kept changing the stones until the water boiled and the meat cooked. Now I knew why her people were called Assiniboins, "stone boilers."

Suns passed and winter came. The snow lay deep on the ground. Alighting Dove helped me make a dress of elkskin. Like my old dress, it was white and a fringe hung from the skirt. But my old dress had long-fringed sleeves and beautiful sky blue quills across the shoulders. The new dress had no sleeves. Instead there was a beaded skin cape that covered the tops of my arms. From beneath the cape hung many ermine tails. The soft fur would keep me warm in the coldest weather. I also had white leggings and moccasins.

As we worked, Alighting Dove told me about her son. He was so swift, she said, that he could run down a buffalo without a horse. He was so strong that he could lift a grizzly bear above his head. He was so brave that he did not hide behind rocks or trees in battle, but rode up to the enemy and dared them to fire at him.

I bowed my head and kept silent. He was also a man without shame, I thought. He had eaten with Swan Necklace and slept in the same tipi. Yet he killed his guest to get a rifle.

When the dress was finished, Alighting Dove called me to the fire. She motioned for me to sit down. Then she took a bone needle and held it in the flame until it glowed. Swiftly, she grabbed my ear and thrust the needle through.

I screamed with pain and grabbed for my ear.

Alighting Dove caught my hand. She shook her head and motioned for me to be still.

Three bright drops of blood fell on my fingers.

Alighting Dove placed a greased stick in the hole to keep it open. Then she did the same to the other ear.

This time I sat quietly and did not make a sound, even when the hot needle went through my ear.

With words and signs, Alighting Dove told me that all Assiniboins had holes in their ears. When the holes were healed I could marry Charging Hawk.

My ears healed too fast. Several times I picked at the wounds to keep them raw. In spite of all I could do, the redness disappeared and the flesh was smooth.

The Assiniboins held a great feast to celebrate the wedding of their chief's son. Fires blazed in the camp.

Drums beat, whistles shrilled, and flutes made soft noises.

After the feasting and dancing and singing, Charging Hawk and I would go to a new tipi. The skins that covered it were painted with buffalo and butterflies, kingfishers and antelope. When I looked at it, I thought of Swan Necklace and my heart was sad.

My sorrow did not show. I put on my new clothes. From my ears hung bangles of silver and blue stones brought from lands far to the south. Alighting Dove said they had cost Charging Hawk three horses.

Because I had no parents to exchange gifts with them, Red Elk and Alighting Dove stood on either side of me and asked for the Great Spirit's blessing. At my feet Charging Hawk laid a beautiful ermine blanket, as white as snow and as soft as a cloud. No one in the tribe had such a beautiful blanket.

"This is our marriage blanket," said Charging Hawk.

"It is beautiful," I said, though my lips were so stiff it was hard to form the Assiniboin words.

Charging Hawk grasped my hands while Red Elk spoke of the wife's duty to her husband and the husband's duty to his wife. He asked the Great Spirit to send us many sons.

The men nodded and the women smiled.

Someone filled a stone pipe with tobacco and

passed it around. Each man took a deep breath and handed it to his neighbor.

Charging Hawk drew deeply on the pipe and blew out the smoke. Then he got to his feet and began to dance. He sang to the beat of the drum and danced about the circle of seated men. He grasped one of the warriors by the hand and pulled him to his feet. Together they danced and sang. One by one, the other men joined them. At last all the men were dancing and singing. The women clapped their hands.

The dancing lasted far into the night. Smoke from the pipes and the fires filled the cold night air. The smoke was so thick that it was hard to see across the circle of dancers.

No one paid any attention to me. I waited. When the dancing grew wild and the voices loud, I snatched the ermine blanket and crept away from the circle.

I crawled through the line of tipis, stopping only to take a rifle and bullets from the tipi of Red Elk. Once I had reached the edge of the village I got to my feet and ran faster than I had ever run before.

Twenty-three

I RAN until I could run no longer. My heart raced and my breath came in great gasps. I bent over and placed my hands on my knees.

When my breathing slowed, I started off again. I walked as fast as I could. I walked until the stars faded and the sky grew light.

I crossed a frozen stream, stepping carefully so that I did not slip. On the far bank I knelt and broke through the ice with a stone. The cold water gave me new strength.

Again I began to walk. The sun warmed me. I would walk until I left this land behind. By evening I would be safe across the border.

I had not gone far when clouds covered the sky. It began to snow. Driven by the wind, the flakes stung my face. It was hard to walk. I dropped into a gully and pulled the ermine blanket over me.

At last the snow stopped and the sky brightened.

When the sun appeared, it had moved the space of my two hands once and then again. It was time to go. Before I could climb out of the gully I heard sounds. I crawled beneath the blanket and waited.

Quietly, I loaded my rifle. Then I lay still, hardly daring to breathe.

A single horse galloped past me.

I peered from beneath the blanket. On its back was Charging Hawk. His eyes were narrowed and his face was grim. If he found me, I would pay dearly for my escape.

While the sun moved across the sky I did not stir. The white blanket blended into the snow. From three steps away, a rider could not see me.

I slept. When I awoke, the shadows were gathering. The sun was low and the first star shone in the sky. With my hands I scraped snow from the ground. I ate only a little, enough to stop my thirst. Still I waited.

At last Charging Hawk returned. His horse gleamed white in the dusk. Charging Hawk was weary from dancing all night and riding all day. His head was on his chest and he no longer looked for me.

He passed the spot where I lay. I reached for my rifle. I peered down the barrel and aimed it with care. When the gun spoke, the bullet would strike him squarely in the back.

Slowly, I began to squeeze the trigger. Then my

eyes filled with the sight of bodies strewn across the ground. I saw the dead people. I saw my mother. I saw Swan Necklace. I saw Ollokot and Fair Land. I saw all our dead chiefs, our dead warriors, our dead women, our dead children. I saw the dead Blue Coats. I saw them as surely as I had seen them at Big Hole and at Bear Paws.

My father's voice spoke in my head. I heard him say, "This hatred sickens my heart. All men were made by the same Great Spirit. Yet we shoot one another down like animals."

My finger fell from the trigger. The rifle slipped from my hand into the snow. I did not pick it up. Some time the killing had to stop.

I had no hate left. I watched Charging Hawk ride out of sight. It was over.

I got to my feet and walked toward the Old Lady's country.

Afterword

SOUND OF RUNNING FEET reached Sitting Bull's camp, where she found White Feather, who had left Bear Paws with White Bird's band. Sound of Running Feet stayed with Sitting Bull for about a year. Then she returned to Lapwai. There she took the name Sarah and married George Moses, another Ne-mee-poo who lived on the reservation. She never saw her father again.

Chief Joseph and the four hundred Ne-mee-poo who surrendered at Bear Paws spent the winter at Fort Leavenworth in Kansas. The land set aside for them lay between a lagoon and the river, and sickness swept through the camp. Many fell ill with malaria. Within a few months, one quarter of the Ne-mee-poo were dead.

The next July they were taken through the summer heat to reservation lands in what today is Oklahoma. The U.S. Army had stripped the Ne-mee-poo of their only source of wealth, their horses, and so they lived in poverty. Nearly fifty more died in the heat of what the Ne-mee-poo called "Eeikish Pah," the Hot Place.

A year later the Ne-mee-poo were moved to another part of Oklahoma, where they spent six years under terrible conditions. Housing was inadequate and medicine virtually nonexistent. Almost every baby born during these six years died. By now, most of the children were dead, including Bending Willow.

Not until 1885 did any of the Ne-mee-poo return to the Lapwai Reservation in Idaho. That spring, all who were willing to become Christians were allowed to return. But Chief Joseph, along with other Ne-mee-poo who refused to embrace a religion they felt had betrayed them, was sent to the Colville Reservation in eastern Washington State. Joseph would never again see the snowy peaks, the blue lake, and the green meadows of Wallowa. He spent the rest of his life at Colville. When he died in 1904, the doctor listed the cause of death as a broken heart.